HIS WOODLAND MAIDEN

SPACE LORDS: A QURILIXEN WORLD NOVEL

MICHELLE M. PILLOW

MICHELLE M. PILLOW® - MICHELLEPILLOW.COM

His Woodland Maiden © copyright 2019 by Michelle M. Pillow

First Printing September 24, 2019, The Raven Books LLC

ISBN-13: 978-1-62501-237-1

Published by The Raven Books LLC

SPACE LORDS SERIES

His Frost Maiden
His Fire Maiden
His Metal Maiden
His Earth Maiden
His Woodland Maiden

ABOUT HIS WOODLAND MAIDEN

SPACE LORDS 5

Space Pirate Rick Hayes flies the high skies searching for mischief. It looks like she finally found him.

From NY Times & USA TODAY Bestselling Author, Michelle M. Pillow, a space adventure romance!

Space pirate and all-around bad boy, Rick Hayes isn't looking to change his ways. He's one helluva pilot, has a crew he thinks of as family, and women seem to want his company. What more could a guy want? Life is too short to settle down, and he knows firsthand the less you care about, the less it hurts when you lose it. Too bad his logic doesn't always get through to his heart. When fate tempts him with a beautiful woman that appears to see through all of his defenses...

Well, actually, the frustrating star beam took him prisoner, hit him over the head, and stole his memories. Regardless of those few minor hiccups on the road to romance, Rick has to decide if love is worth the risk.

A Qurilixen World Novel
Space Pirates, Science Fiction Romance

MichellePillow.com

WELCOME TO QURILIXEN

Qurilixen World Novels

Dragon Lords Series
Barbarian Prince
Perfect Prince
Dark Prince
Warrior Prince
His Highness The Duke
The Stubborn Lord
The Reluctant Lord
The Impatient Lord
The Dragon's Queen

Lords of the Var® Series

The Savage King
The Playful Prince
The Bound Prince
The Rogue Prince
The Pirate Prince

Captured by a Dragon-Shifter Series

Determined Prince
Rebellious Prince
Stranded with the Cajun
Hunted by the Dragon
Mischievous Prince
Headstrong Prince

Space Lords Series

His Frost Maiden
His Fire Maiden
His Metal Maiden
His Earth Maiden
His Woodland Maiden

AUTHOR UPDATES

To stay informed about when a new book is released sign up for updates:

http://michellepillow.com/author-updates/

Dear Readers,

Rick finally met his match!

I know we've all been waiting to see what kind of woman would take this bad boy pilot down. Don't worry, she'll keep him on his naughty little toes. I'm so excited-nervous-excited that release day is finally here!

I'm also a little sad. This is the last planned book in the Space Lords series installment. I love this crew. But, not to worry, I'm sure they'll make appearances in other Qurilixen World novels.

I hope you all know what the Qurilixen World is by now, but if not it is a collection of several series within the Qurilixen story world. If you're new to my work—you are in for an exciting reading treat!

This may be the last planned Space Lords series

book, but that doesn't mean the space adventures are over. I have several ideas in the works for more series installments. *squee* By the end of this book, you might be able to guess one of the ideas.

Thank you, readers, for loyally flying the high skies with this mischievous crew. I'm sorry Rick is now taken, but he might have a doppelganger or two flying out there looking for love. So watch out if you're outside at night and see a spaceship. It just might be a bad boy pirate looking for some intergalactic love.

Happy Reading!
Michelle M. Pillow

PROLOGUE

Lin Yao Mines, Planet of Lintian

Rick Hayes couldn't remember most of the journey to the purple jade mines, but he remembered her. He didn't have a name for *her*. She hadn't given him one before hitting him over the head and taking him prisoner.

The smell of dank earth filled each breath. At least they'd put him on a portable chair and not the rocky ground. It wasn't luxury, but it was something. His eyes had long adjusted to the dim lights strung across the mine's ceiling. It cast the jagged edges of the stone walls into contrast. His hands worked against his ties. He knew very little about this planet and had no way of knowing what manner of creatures called Lintian home. So, when he escaped it should prove interesting.

Her, otherwise known as the dark-haired enchantress, had smiled at him while they were docked on Leinad's star port where they'd stopped for fuel. He knew the look of feminine invitation and assumed she wanted him to follow her as she left the bar. It was only after he pursued her into some kind of criminal meet-n-greet that he realized his assumption might have been wrong. Being a space pirate himself, Rick usually fit right into such questionable situations. This had not been one of those times.

Rick and his crew had been on their way to Qurilixen, the homeworld of their ship's captain. Prince (aka Captain) Jarek's family ruled half of the planet, so they were always treated like royalty when they visited—soft beds, endless food, drinking, and gaming. Unmated females were rare, so it did lack one thing. Still, a soft bed would be better than being trussed up like a human sacrifice.

"The bosses aren't going to like this," he heard one of the men whisper from an adjoining tunnel. The rest of the kidnappers hadn't given their names either. "This pirate doesn't factor into our plans. We should have killed him before leaving the star port."

Rick had been able to figure out he was being held by intergalactic drug traders. For the most part, his abductors had made it very clear they wanted to kill him. It was only the woman who'd kept him alive.

Rick tried to suppress his grin. Not surprising since he did have a way with the ladies.

Currently they were near some place called the Lin Yao Mines located in Singhai near the Shan Gung Din palace. The information meant little to him except where there was a civilization there would be a ship he could steal to escape the planet. Rick could fly pretty much anything.

His crew would come for him… if they knew where to look. Since he'd been unconscious when the enchantress' ship left the star port, he wasn't sure if his friends knew who'd taken him. That meant he was on his own until proven otherwise.

A series of loud thuds sounded from the tunnel. He craned his neck and tried to jerk his feet free from the binds. The drug dealing enchantress appeared in the yellowed light. Blue lines encased her dark eyes. Only, her gaze wasn't sparkling with mischief like he'd grown accustomed to seeing. She came to him in a panic.

"Change of plans," she whispered, digging in the pouch at her thigh only to pull out a syringe.

"Oh, hold on babycakes, there's no reason to do anything rash." Rick leaned away from her hand, not knowing what kind of threat was in the syringe.

"We've come so far. No reason to resort to killing me now."

"I had planned on wiping your mind and leaving you on some remote fueling dock with a couple of hundred credits so your space pirate buddies could find you, but it looks like I'll have to do this our normal way."

"What do you mean our normal way? We have a normal way?" He pushed his feet against the floor, trying to move the chair and unable to get it to do more than rock back and forth.

"I know you won't remember this, but you need to stop following me, Rick. I hope this thought embeds deeply in your mind. If you see me, walk the other way. I can't keep saving you. This has to be the last time." She licked her lips.

"What are you talking—?"

The words were cut off as she pressed her mouth to his. She kissed him deeply, grasping the back of his head with one hand. It wasn't a sweet, testing kiss, but one from a woman who'd done this to him before. Surely, he'd remember such a thing. Her touch felt familiar. His body responded instantly, and he groaned, fighting against his ties.

A sharp jab pierced his thigh, but he hardly cared. When she pulled back, breathing as hard as he, Rick tried to follow her mouth to continue.

She put her hand to his lips to stop him and

said, "You won't remember this, but I am sorry. Good luck."

Rick blinked hard. She threw the syringe down a dark crevice and turned toward the tunnel where her men were.

"Release him," a loud voice ordered. Rick detected a flash of red trimmed in gold as a man entered the cave. More was said, but the words became muffled as his vision darkened. He felt his body slumping forward but was too weak to stop it.

"Wake up." A hard slap pulled Rick from the darkness.

He flung his arms, trying to remember where he was and how he'd gotten there. He sat on a hard floor, pressed against an uneven wall. A sharp, jagged rock poked his back. Golden firelight burned from a torch, revealing the corners of the dark cave walls.

His cheek stung as he glanced around the cave only to focus on a woman tied to a chair. The memories were foggy, but he knew that face—his kidnapper from Leinad's star port.

What was going on?

"Who are you?" Rick turned his attention to the man who'd presumably rescued him. He wore loose red pants and a black silk tunic shirt. It hardly looked like what one would wear spelunking.

Using the rock wall for support, he pulled

himself to his feet. Rick's thigh ached, and he felt weak.

Seriously, what had happened?

"I am Prince Zhang Haun of the Muntong Empire, heir to the Zhang throne," the man answered, though he spoke in the Old Star language his accent matched that of a few of the drug queen-pin's men.

They were on Lintian. He was starting to remember.

Sort of.

The prince's companions—guards maybe—were standing out of the way in a tunnel. It was impossible to tell how many there were.

"What exactly is happening?" Rick moved on wobbly legs to look down at his former captor all tied up. She glared at him, although a gag kept her from speaking.

"I was hoping you could tell me," the prince said. "What is she doing here?"

Rick opened his mouth to answer but couldn't. He frowned. The answer was right on the edge of his thoughts, but he couldn't form it.

The woman began an angry tirade of words muffled by the gag in her mouth.

"Oh, babycakes, don't be angry," Rick said, stroking the woman's hair. He leaned closer to whisper, "Look who's tied up now. Be a good girl, and maybe I'll save you from this predicament."

The animated tirade only continued as she tried to say something to him, thrusting her sexy body against the ties.

The prince merely watched.

Rick wasn't sure who to trust. Considering the situation, he thought it best to play on the side of the prince. Plus, it was too much to resist taunting the enchantress as she had him.

"I believe you told me to behave when I was in your situation." Rick patted her on the head, which only irritated her more. "Though I do understand that behaving is such a broad term, open to interpretation. When I said I'd behave, I didn't say how."

She slammed her feet against the stone ground. Her chair lifted by small degrees. Her expressive eyes said more than her mouth ever could.

"Ah, sweet cheeks," Rick touched his chest, "you're breaking my heart."

She stopped moving, though her glare remained.

"I'm not sure what I am witnessing," the prince admitted, his words low. "Why were she and the others keeping you here?"

"Can I assume I have you to thank for rescuing me?" Rick asked.

The man nodded. "Though I'm not sure it was much of a rescue. They did not put up a fight."

"Is that so?" Rick turned toward the queenpin. There was plenty he'd wanted to say to her, only he couldn't recall what at the moment. Maybe he'd hit his head? His thoughts were fuzzy. The smart thing would be to worry about his own escape, but he couldn't bring himself to abandon her. He had no idea what would happen to her if he left her with the prince. To Haun, he said, "This prisoner is mine. I'll make sure she gets off this planet and never bothers you again."

How he wasn't sure.

The prince began to protest, but Rick talked over him.

"Frankly, honey pie, I'm disappointed in you," Rick said to her. "All this time and you were so easy to catch off guard. What? Nothing to say now? No smartass command? No snide remarks? It's not fun being tied to a chair, is it?"

She yelled and pitched her body forward as if to headbutt him. His boot slid as he caught her and kept her from falling.

"We are not going to get answers this way." The prince lifted his hand to stop any protest that might come. "As soon as my men return with a mode of transport, we will take her to the prisons and you will come with us until we can figure out what is happening—"

A roar interrupted his words, echoing from the tunnel opposite of where the prince's men waited.

Rick and the prince turned in surprise.

"Holy space balls!" Rick exclaimed seeing Jarek halfway shifted into the form of an upright man-cat. Within seconds the captain could become a full tiger. Claws, fur, and fangs created a scary-ass figure. His arm was pulled back, ready to strike. Rick rubbed his eyes in surprise. "Captain? Is that really you?"

Jarek's gaze darted over the room.

"Rick?" Jarek lowered his arm, stopping his aggressive attack plans. It wasn't clear if it was confusion or relief that the man felt. "You're... free? How? I don't understand."

Rick had never been so happy to see someone in his life. He rushed to Jarek and threw his arms around him. "Blessed stars, Jarek, it's good to see you. How did you ever find me?"

"You should've known I would." Jarek pushed him away. "How did you get free? What is going on here? I come expecting a rescue, and I see you tormenting some woman..." His words tapered off as his eyes moved toward the prince.

"Oh, yeah, sorry, Cap. This is Prince Zhang Haun of the, uh, Moon Empire," Rick said.

"Muntong," Haun corrected.

"Right, right, Muntong." Rick grinned, patting Prince Haun on the back. He had no clue what he'd forgotten but was happy this ordeal appeared to be almost over. The prince stiffened at the familiar contact, but Rick ignored the reaction. "Anyway, ole Haun here saved my sorry ass. He said we were waiting for someone, but I never thought he meant you. I thought it was my lucky day."

He couldn't wait to be free of the mines.

"Sacred Cats, Rick, you need a bath." Jarek wrinkled his nose.

Rick glanced down at his dirty, tattered clothing, and then at the woman tied to the chair. He felt a mix of emotions when he looked at her—confusion and lust being the most prevalent.

"Jarek?" a woman's soft voice questioned as she joined the captain. She was a pretty, slender little thing.

"*Meimei*," Haun said.

The woman ran toward the prince, wrapping her arms around him.

"Who's that?" Rick whispered, thinking his crew had kidnapped the woman to exchange for his safe return. "His woman?"

"That is Princess Mei, his sister. We had her on our ship. She helped us find these mines."

"Don't tell me you kidnapped her in exchange

for me." Rick arched a brow. If it was true, they were all idiots. Kidnapping royalty was never a well-conceived idea. He and the rest of the pirate crew had learned that lesson. Though, by the way Mei hugged her brother, all was well this time.

Rick felt dizzy and wanted nothing more than to leave the mines. All that mattered was his freedom, the fact his crew had found him, and he was going back where he belonged—off the planet and into the high skies.

HARPER VIRANT PEERED through a seam in the spaceship's ceiling at the two idiots below. They lounged in the ship's commons, one draping his limbs over a chair and the other a couch. Loud sighs and long pauses in their conversation attested to the men's boredom. A cleaning droid buzzed and clanked between them as it rolled over the floor. Its numerous repairs evident by the piecemeal way it was put together.

The ship had not left the planet, so they were still on Lintian's surface, but it had moved away from the purple jade mines, where they had apprehended her. Since Princess Mei was with the crew, that probably meant they had landed in Muntong territory. There had been some conversation about returning a map to Mei's family.

Not that it mattered to Harper. No one would be coming to her rescue regardless of what side of the planet she was on. Not this time.

"You should have let me pull for myself," Lucien said, referring to when they'd drawn lots to determine who would stay with her on the ship. He was a pale, thin alien with red-brown eyes. A bowl of tiny, round food pieces rested on his stomach, and he absently dropped them in front of the droid to force it to move back and forth to clean the mess. "Why did you have to bring me into your bad luck? Now I'm stuck here guarding a drug queenpin with you instead of venturing on-world."

They still thought she was a queenpin dealing the drug *chandoo*, which was being produced in the Lin Yao Mines. That was something, at least. The truth was, she hated *chandoo* and what it did to people. It lured the user in, made them feel alive, but eventually would rot their brain and leave them little more than a worthless mass of nothingness. Luckily, one of the local royal families was fighting hard to destroy the drug, and production would hopefully be stopped. At least at the Lintian site.

Once she was off this ship, the odds of her crossing paths with this crew again should have been almost nil. But, for some strange reason, Rick kept popping up in her life like a bad luck charm and she had to keep taking his memories from him. This time she was dealing with his entire crew and didn't have the means to erase herself from their minds. Hopefully, if they tried looking for a queenpin, they'd never track her. After today, she'd become someone else.

"You're just mad that you won't see what Princess Mei's sister looks like," Viktor answered. He appeared to be of the same alien classification as Lucien, but with green-red eyes. They bickered like brothers, and by their looks she assumed they might be related. From what she'd gathered as they brought her on board, Viktor was a mechanic, and Lucien was in charge of the ship's communications. There was also a security officer named Jackson who moved like an elite soldier. She could see the training a mile away. Thankfully, he had not been left to guard her. She highly doubted she'd be in the process of escaping so soon if that were the case.

"Rick should be the one looking after the prisoner. She kidnapped *him*, not us," Lucien continued complaining. "Why does he want to take her with us, anyway? We should leave her with the emperor. Let them deal with the lowlife. I'm surprised they agreed to let us take her."

Lowlife? Harper frowned. That was rich coming from space pirates.

"I think Mei arranged it." Viktor gave a small laugh. "What do you think the queenpin did to him? Rick looked pretty shaken. I don't think I've ever seen him that upset before. There has to be a reason why he wants to keep her."

"She probably gave the rocket boy attention." Lucien chuckled. "He did trail after her like a lost semikin."

"Rick in love," Viktor snorted. "Can you imagine?"

"Sure." Lucien grinned, craning his neck to look at the other man. "He tells himself he loves himself every chance he gets."

"Seriously, though," Viktor insisted, "it's not like we're going to ransom her back to her criminal family."

"Maybe she has something else of value." Lucien threw a handful of food on the floor for the droid.

"Maybe she was trying to kill him." Viktor rubbed the heel of his hand against his eye. "I honestly didn't think we'd find him alive. I didn't want to say it, but I thought we were on some kind of revenge mission."

"We might still be," Lucien answered.

Harper had never intended to kidnap Rick, but he'd shown up at the worst possible time, and she'd had two options—take him or kill him. The fact that his crew came after him was about the best possible scenario. Otherwise, she wasn't sure how much longer she could have kept the smartass alive. The life of a space pirate ranked low on her bosses' list of concerns, and he was more trouble than he was worth.

Satisfied that her guards didn't act concerned with checking on her at the moment, Harper crawled through the ceiling of the ship. A thick layer of dust covered old engine parts and abandoned pipes. A metal box was wedged next to a grate. There wasn't a lid, and it appeared to be a collection of holo-discs. Someone on the crew was trying to hide their stash of contraband.

Most of the light came from the halls beneath, casting a soft glow through the seams, cracks, and removable grates. The few times she lifted the grates was to find she was over sleeping quarters. Ship designs had been uploaded into her brain, but unfortunately, this particular class of ship wasn't one of them, so she had to guess her route. She turned around when she came to the metal construct of a VR. The wires and control panels needed to run the virtual reality room created a thick jungle that she couldn't squeeze through.

Her pants snagged on a piece of jagged metal, slicing through the thick material to cut her upper thigh. This was not her finest escape.

Harper frowned and automatically felt the wound. Her fingers slid in blood. The injury wasn't critical, but it would need attention sooner rather than later. She picked up her pace, ignoring the pain. The last thing she wanted was to spend the rest of eternity as a skeleton stuck in the ceiling panels of a pirate ship.

2

*Virtual Reality Advanced Technology and Programming
Conference, Planet of Nozando, Several Years Later…*

A technical conference focusing on virtual reality programming code sounded like the beginning of a promising nap. Rick Hayes had only agreed to land there for a few reasons. First, being the pilot of the *Bound Virgin*, he pretty much had to go wherever the captain told him. Second, since their ship was a flying piece of reconstructed—*um*—beauty, they needed to scavenge parts wherever they could find them to keep her going. This conference was a treasure trove of free (and questionably free) gifts. Third, being a space pirate sailing the high skies in hope of an adventure wasn't as glamorous as it sounded. New VR programs would go a long way toward alleviating months of boredom floating in space—not that the married crew members would agree to the type of VR programs he had in mind.

"What they don't know, they don't know," Rick said to himself. Then, grinning, he thought, *Maybe they'd be into it. I've never been married. Who am I to judge?*

Tickets to this thing were difficult to acquire and very exclusive. Lucien, who was in charge of the ship's communications, had intercepted a transmission wave about a Trogarthian game of chance. That was how Lucien had ended up winning the VR crew pass for the conference.

"Nice space-trash costume," a man called to Dev, laughing.

Rick hid his smirk. Dev was dressed in his usual garb—all black and ready for battle. The jokester was brave, if stupid. The half-Bevlon, half-human man could have thrown him across the pavilion without breaking a sweat. Dev's father had been a demon. Well, the equivalent of a demon, anyway.

"What are you smiling about?" Dev glanced back to Rick from where he walked with his wife, Violette Stephans. "He was talking about you, rocket boy."

"Don't take it personally, big fella. I think you're handsome." Rick winked at him.

Dev was their ship's head of security. Well, he was if anyone bothered to look at their ship logs. As long as credential codes cleared upon landing and they had their passes, no one at these events wanted to upset their wealthy clientele by digging around in their records. They wanted them to be happy because happy rich people spent an insane amount of space credits upgrading VR units and buying programs.

It was only after he'd followed Dev through the docking lot to the main pavilion that he'd figured out his fourth (and best) reason for coming.

Ladies.

"Come to Rick, babycakes." Rick grinned as two women walked past in tight black skinsuits with bright blue gun belts slung around their waists. They each had patches of fake yellow fur glued down the center of their foreheads. They were into roleplaying. What a coincidence, so was he. "What planet are you from? Because you're breaking a dozen intergalactic treaties just walking around with bodies like that. You looking for someone to play…?"

The women ignored him, and he let his come-on line fade away. They went to a portable VR display labeled "Fur Play" and held up the back of their hands to show where metal chips had been embedded into their flesh. The hairy vendor scanned them, and seconds later the door to the VR slid open. A bright light flashed as strange animal noises sounded from within.

Rick quickened his pace, hurrying to get a glimpse inside as the women entered. Thick foliage blocked the view, and the door closed before he could detect anything remotely fun. No matter, there were plenty of other things to look at.

The organizers had set up portable VR booths. The small metal domes formed rows that flanked four open walkways; two walkways on each side of an enclosed hallway down the center aisle. Apparently, the adventure tunnel, as the central VR enclosure was being referred to, was the highlight of the show. It consisted of multiple, highly interactive displays. A line of people waited to go inside. According to the holographic map floating near him, the enclosure let out in the auditorium where there would be a keynote speaker later—some boring scientist type with an even more boring name. Rick would not be attending the lecture.

"Did I honestly just hear you say to those women that they're breaking a dozen intergalactic treaties just walking around with bodies like that?" Violette arched a brow as she and Dev caught up to him.

"Sounds like Rick has been practicing ways to

talk to women again," Dev answered in his usually dry tone.

"He does need all the help he can get." Violette directed her comment to Dev but obviously said it for Rick's benefit.

"How else will he end the curse?" Dev agreed.

"Maybe you should give him some pointers." Violette smiled up at her husband.

Rick hated hearing about the stupid curse and wished his crewmates would let it drop already. So what if he'd pissed off some spirit? Out of the five men who'd been hit with Zhang An's wrath, he was the only one yet to break her curse. What they never considered was, he didn't necessarily *want* to break it. He was fine being a bachelor.

After being taken prisoner by a drug queenpin and dragged through the far reaches of space, something Rick still wasn't sure how he survived, he and five others from their crew had been taken to meet Emperor Zhang. Captain Jarek had been in charge then, and during Rick's rescue the catshifter had fallen in love with the emperor's daughter. It was not a union that was met with celebration on the planet of Lintian. The emperor and his wife were upset. An ancestral spirit had shown up and stirred emotions even more. The situation had been tense.

Rick's brain had been a little jumbled from whatever had happened in the mines and so maybe his judgment had been off at the time. Regardless, being his naturally charismatic self, he'd tried to ease the tension by making a joke, and five of them ended up cursed. Jarek escaped it because he'd already fallen in love with Mei. Rick and fellow crewmen Jackson, Dev, Evan, and Lochlann had not been so lucky. Lucien and Viktor only escaped because they'd been stuck on the spaceship poorly guarding the prisoner who had escaped on their watch.

Zhang An's curse had to do with finding love under the guise of the Lintianese elements of water, fire, metal, wood, and earth. As far as curses went, it wasn't all that scary.

What had she said?

"Together you travel and together you'll remain. Tied and joined like the five elements of our people."

Something, something, roads, happiness, underwear, dying alone.

"You will find your love hidden within the mystery of the five elements. One element for each of you. The corresponding element will hold the secret to your future happiness. But fate is not clear. If you do not recognize it, you will lose it and be forever alone."

The prediction itself wasn't the curse. It was the

not knowing which element for which person, and what all that gibberish about the elements even meant. The old spirit had given just enough clues to consume their thoughts without saying anything useful.

If anything, the cursed crewmen should be thanking him. It could be argued that his curse helped the others be prepared for love once it showed up. Evan was now living off-world with his wife Josselyn, a woman they had saved from a stone prison—literally she'd been encased in stone.

That led to Dev being taken by Josselyn's estranged sister, Violette. They'd fallen in love and gotten married. The couple currently walked in front of him.

Their new captain, Lochlann, had met Alexis thanks to Rick sneaking her onto their ship. Captain Lochlann was a dragonshifter from Qurilixen and Alexis's past was, well, complicated. Yet again, another couple happily mated.

Which left Jackson, who worked closely with Dev doing ship security. He had most recently fallen in love with Raisa. She programmed food simulators, creating recipes on a molecular level. He had never eaten so well in all his years flying the high skies. She was also part Angelion, which meant she had a way with mechanical devices and electricity.

She could read the inside of a ship just by touching the wall in front of it.

Rick grinned. Four out of five parts of the curse broken. They should be thanking him, not teasing him. He was like an intergalactic matchmaker.

No, he was like a love god.

Oh, yeah.

Love god. He liked the sound of that.

"I think we hurt his feelings," Violette said. "Rick? You still with us, buddy?"

Rick realized he'd gone off into his own thoughts. Everything around the time he'd been rescued from the mines bothered him. With the sole purpose of aggravating Dev, he said, "I was just wondering about something."

Dev had the sense of humor of a rock sometimes. Rick assumed it had something to do with the demonic upbringing of his father's people. Bevlons had a torture-is-love parenting style. Then again, so did a lot of parents. At least the Bevlons admitted it.

"I'm waiting," Dev answered.

Rick stepped closer to Violette and fell into stride next to her. "Vi, do you think it's because your father was a general that you ended up with a guy like Dev?"

Violette arched a brow. Her green eyes studied him as if waiting for the rest.

"I hear women often marry men who remind them of their fathers. Is that why you chose Mr. Personality over me? You were raised on a military base, and he's all about discipline? You got daddy issues?"

It worked. Dev scowled.

Rick wasn't surprised when Violette took a swing at him. Her punch wasn't as forceful as it could have been, and he was able to duck out of the way.

Rick winked at her as he put distance between them so she couldn't swing again. "Easy, love, you know I'm just jealous you chose him over me."

"Stop flirting with my wife," Dev stated, his tone flat.

"Was that flirting?" Violette asked, caressing Dev's chest. "I couldn't tell. See, I think he does need you to teach him how to talk to women. He'll never meet someone at the rate he's going."

Rick pretended to be wounded by her comment.

She looked pointedly at Rick. "And I have no issue with who my father was."

They both knew that was a lie. The general had been a complicated man.

"You two have fun. Try not to impregnate any Murkernals." Rick spun away before giving his friend time to respond, intent on disappearing into the crowd. Dev had innocently given fruit to an alien species, and they'd instantly procreated to the point their population doubled. It was a story they liked to remind Dev of often.

"I just gave them fruit—" Dev started to protest, but his words were cut off by the murmur of conversations coming from the surrounding crowd.

Rick wanted to be lost in the crowd, alone in a sea of distractions. He needed to be surrounded by something other than the happy couples on the ship. Yes, he liked being a bachelor, but as one of only three single men remaining of the crew, it was getting harder and harder to go anywhere on board where he wasn't met with paired-off unions. He didn't begrudge the marriages, but there were enough kissing sessions and suggestive whispers to remind him he crawled into bed alone at night.

A man could only romance himself so many times.

Groups of aliens passed by him. Their appearances used to draw his notice, the extra eyes and bony protrusions, but it was rare that anything surprised him anymore. A woman with yellow reptilian skin narrowed her eyes at him and appeared to be ready to do battle. Her oval head flared out at the cheeks, widening her features. She undoubtedly reacted to the fact he'd smiled at her.

Rick waggled his brow and suggestively glanced toward a nearby VR pod. Her long tongue slithered out, and she hurried away from him as if he were the ugliest invitation to sex she had ever received.

He couldn't help but laugh.

For Rick, smiling was as natural as breathing. The expression was on his face regardless of what he felt inside. No one needed to know what he was truly feeling at any given moment for, whatever bad emotions filled him, they would soon be buried deep where no one could find them. In many ways, existence was a fluid, pointless thing.

A life spent sailing the high skies had taught him one thing. It wasn't that life was short, or that everyone's time was limited, or that the endlessness of deep space became tedious after months in the black. It was that in the grand scheme of everything, what he did mattered. Some greater force out there didn't seem to want him dead. It wasn't for lack of his trying. When he was younger, he'd put himself in all kinds of stupid situations, ones that no humanoid should get out of, and he kept surviving. Now that he was older, he put himself in even more dangerous situations, only for better reasons (mostly). His risky lifestyle was as good a reason as any to remain single.

He was one damned lucky fly boy.

He'd be even luckier if he managed to score some amazing VR equipment while at the conference. If not for filling the lonely time adrift, then for helping to keep him from dwelling on his past. Rick hated to dwell. The past couldn't be changed, so he found no reason to let his thoughts wander in that direction. The future was uncertain. Now is what mattered. He needed to focus on what was happening right in front of him.

"Rick, you have to try the adventure hall." Viktor approached, looking very much like a cadet who'd just been introduced to a Galaxy Playmate for the first time. His brother Lucien was behind him, trying not to look excited even though it was evident that he was. The brothers were half-human, half-Dere. Their blanched complexions were nearly identical.

"You'll love it. They have Old Earth scenes in there," Lucien said. It was no secret Rick had a mild obsession for twenty-first-century Old Earth memorabilia. "Just make sure the safety override is turned on when you go through so everything remains a hologram. If the override is shut off, the tunnel is fully interactive until everyone who went inside is finished with their tour."

"Sounds more fun that way," Rick dismissed the warning.

"Seriously, don't. Once you go in you can't turn back," Lucien warned. "There are some creatures even Jackson and Dev wouldn't want to face. We watched a Syog emerge covered in strange bites. Another guy was floated out by a medic stretcher."

"Any luck scavenging for programs?" Rick asked.

"Not yet." Viktor worked as their mechanic. To his credit, the man could rig almost anything, including a scanner that could (theoretically) bypass security protocols and record VR programs.

"He's been too busy exploring," Lucien admitted.

"*We've* been too busy," Viktor corrected. "Forget deep space travel. I want to live here."

"They clear out the pods when this is over," Lucien said. "Though it's too bad we can't stay. I hear the Medical Alliance conference is coming up. We could undoubtedly scavenge some new tech at that one. It's not like anyone can afford to buy most of the stuff they sell, anyway. The markup on medical booths is out of this galaxy outlandish."

By scavenge, of course, they meant steal but the word had a nicer ring to it.

"And they call *us* pirates," Rick muttered. The Medical Alliance for Planetary Health (MAPH) had direct ties to the Medical Mafia. Together they controlled nearly everything from medical booths to scientific studies to galactic drug supplies. The crew had run-ins with both groups more times than they cared to think about.

"I think we can all agree to stay off the mafia's radar," Viktor said. "Captain was clear. No mafia, no Federation Military, no Larceny Casino, no—"

"What's left?" Rick frowned, thinking over every less-than-upstanding organization they'd tangled with in the last few years. "Are we going to start flying vacation transports to Quazer? Next, you'll be saying the Galaxy Playmate ship is off-limits. I draw the line there."

"Captain can't do that," Lucien said before turning to his brother, looking horrified at the idea they might no longer be permitted access to ships full of beautiful women. "Tell me he won't do that."

"There's supposed to be a Galaxy Playmates VR world somewhere around here. Keep an eye out." Viktor patted his jacket pocket. "I'm going to try to scan the programming and see if I can get a copy for us."

Rick understood Viktor's excitement. VR companionship would be better than watching sexy Old Earth transmissions on the viewing screen in his quarters. At least the women would hold a conversation with him, even if it was programmed.

Rick placed his hand on Viktor's shoulder. "It's a

noble and dangerous mission ahead of you, friend, and I promise *if you succeed*, I will not leave you behind. Even if the entire security team is trying to kill you."

"Thanks—Wait, what if I try and I *don't* succeed, and the security team tries to kill me?" Viktor asked.

"Well, it will have been swell knowing you. We will miss you, and I'll wish you the best of luck in your escape." Rick grinned, walking a few paces backward. "By the way, if you fail, when they're chasing you, try to make it out of the pavilion. I hear the mountain folk on this planet are very welcoming to newcomers. They hardly ever sacrifice them."

Lucien laughed as Viktor grumbled a response.

Rick made his way toward the center of the pavilion. The stone floors were polished smooth, and the glass arches of the ceiling let in enough outside light that not much else was needed. Metal seams held the panes into place. Occasionally, the shadow of a security drone would cross his path.

He scanned the crowd, looking for potential problems. It was an old habit, but one that had kept him alive more than once.

Everyone walked around in pairs or groups. They didn't seem the least bit bothered by the increased security at the conference. They were all in their own little worlds, hardly noticing anyone or anything around them.

"Did you see the rendering of the hogbeast? I've fought many and I doubt the programmer has even seen one in real life," a woman with small horns protruding from her head like a crown boasted to her friends. She had the leather-plated clothing of someone who found herself in trouble more often than not.

Rick could relate.

"I want the one with the triangle bed." A humanoid woman stroked her hands down the white feather wings of her partner as they came from the opposite direction.

The Angelion lifted his wings slightly to shake her off. "I'll bet you do. I saw the way you eyed those two servants holding the pot of oil."

"But watching torture is so much fun," she persisted. "Please?"

Rick made a mental note. A full-blooded Angelion at the same event as Dev could be a problem later. Although a good brawl would be a fun way to alleviate boredom. Bevlons and Angelions went together like angels and demons. Incidentally, since half-Bevlon Dev and half-Angelion Raisa both had a human parent, their proximity had never caused a problem on the ship.

The woman glanced back to look over the

crowd, hate in her eyes. Her gaze met Rick's and narrowed.

Second mental note, the female torturer was more of a threat.

He again searched the crowd as he made his way toward the adventure tunnel line. The faintest melody of a laugh caught his attention. It sent chills of recognition over him. He knew that voice. He thought about that voice often.

As if in a trance, he followed the sound, looking for the source. A memory tried to pull itself from the murky trenches of his mind. It was the place where all the pains he did not allow himself to feel lived.

A woman moved past him. Her dark hair coiled around the crown of her head. A thin veil covered the locks. She turned to the side. He saw the line of her neck and the angle of her jaw as the sheer fabric rippled with movement.

It was enough. He remembered her.

She had not given him an actual name, so his memories had nothing to call her.

She didn't look like herself, not like when she'd sauntered around her ship's prison cell and threatened to eject him into the deep black. Now her clothes were demure, thick and flowing, almost laughably so considering she was a drug dealer. Even so, she was the same woman who'd abducted him years before and had taken him to the Lin Yao Mines on the planet of Lintian.

There was something about her the first time he'd seen her on Leinad's star port that had made him want to follow. She moved with confidence as if she belonged in her surroundings. Her body had flowed through the crowd. He'd tried to talk to her, to get her attention, to see why she was different from the other women he'd seen. His heart had been beating so fast, so hard. He wanted her, the surge inside his body like a blast from a starship. Her eyes had locked on his and then... nothing.

All emotion had disappeared. He remembered what happened next with the same dispassion he recalled the food menu at a fuel dock diner. He'd followed her into a private room and right into a drug deal. The painted metal walls had been a strange backdrop to the twinkling of the floating chandeliers as if the proprietors had tried to dress up a sinking ship. Guns had been drawn. He'd made some wiseass remark as he'd tried to back out. The woman had struck him over the head, surprisingly strong. He'd woken up restrained in a chair.

All that, and he felt nothing.

Rick considered himself a fairly easygoing guy, but he had to admit the lack of emotional memory was strange. Sure the actions were there, but that was it. No hint that he'd felt anything during it whatsoever. When he was passed out, it was possible they'd done something to him to take away his feelings, but the medical booth scans had revealed nothing.

In the end, it didn't matter. His crew had found him. He'd escaped her, then she'd escaped him. He'd moved on from that adventure to the next, and then the next, and then…

It was her. She was here.

Rick found himself compelled to follow. It was curiosity. No, it was more than that. It wasn't lust, at least not purely. He was a man who enjoyed female company, after all, so of course he was attracted to her. It was an itching in his brain, a tingling in his nerves. It was a thought on the cusp of being born, but still elusive.

The high coil of her hair acted like a beacon to guide him. He found himself weaving through the crowd, lifting his arm to part groups when they would block his path. Something whispered in his mind to turn around, to leave it in the past.

Rick was never very good at listening to that inner voice.

He reached her side and took her gently by the elbow. "Miss me, moonbeam?"

The woman jerked away from him in surprise before turning around. Dark eyes met his and filled with panic. Another memory tried to surface, and he imagined he was standing in a forest. As fast as it came, it left.

"I don't know you," she answered, her tone firm. "You have the wrong person."

"That hurts, starshine. I—" His words were cut off when the brute she was with placed a heavy hand on Rick's shoulder.

"Eloise, is this space debris bothering you?" the brute demanded.

Rick shrugged away from the touch. Why hadn't he taken note of her companion?

Eloise? That was her name?

The brute roughly shoved Eloise behind him and straightened his broad shoulders. By appearance he was humanoid, a thick, muscled, ill-tempered humanoid.

Rick glanced around to see if any of his crew were nearby. This man was as tall as Dev. Any fight that erupted wouldn't be a fair one.

Rick's concern was for Eloise. What had he walked into? She didn't appear too happy to be pushed around by her companion. A feeling of protectiveness rose up inside him.

"No, Bucky, he's mistaken." Despite the irritated expression on her face as she stood behind the man, Eloise's tone was demure as she tried to pull him away with her. "Come, I want to see the adventure tunnel—"

There was no way Rick was going to leave her alone with this guy. Every inner alarm he had went off at the idea. Bucky radiated danger—and not the good kind.

"That hurts, babycakes, after all that time we spent alone together on Lintian," Rick interrupted, unable to stop himself. "I thought you said you loved me."

"What? I never!" Eloise again tried to pull Bucky. "He's joking with you. I've never been to Lintian."

Bucky's eyes widened, and he demanded, "You are not pure?"

A drug queenpin would have lived anything but a pure life. Why was she pretending to be anything but who she was?

"I've been cloistered on—"

Eloise tried to answer but the beast of a man moved as if to grab her.

"Pure? Her?" Rick forced a laugh to draw the man's attention away from the woman. Yeah, he'd stepped into something strange this time. None of this made sense.

The faint sound of hydraulics caught his attention as Bucky faced Rick once more. There was a mechanical look to the way Bucky's shirt cut against his shoulder as if his arm was encased in metal and tubes instead merely of muscled flesh. Rick glanced down to see the man's bionic hand balling into a fist. Someone had sprayed a silicone layer over the metal frame, but the wiring was unmistakable.

Suddenly, Rick *was* worried.

Sacred space balls, this was going to hurt.

Bucky's arm cocked back, ready to strike. Rick tried to stumble back but bumped into someone from the crowd. He lifted his hands to protect his face.

"Blast it, Rick," Eloise swore. She reached for the back of Bucky's sleeves and pulled.

Two loud pops sounded, and green ooze dripped down as the man's arms instantly dropped uselessly to his sides. The move saved Rick from a potentially lethal fate.

Eloise jerked Bucky's shoulder, tripping him with an outstretched leg. As the man fell, her eyes met Rick's and she scowled. "You better get out of here. Prince Bucky's bodyguards won't be too far behind."

Bucky rolled back and forth on the floor, sputtering curse words. He spun on his back and tried to kick Eloise without getting up. The sound of running feet and excited murmurings gave credence to her warning.

Rick didn't hesitate as he followed Eloise. She cut through the line of people waiting for their turn through the adventure hall. The automatic door opened to invite the next guests to pass through. Eloise pushed a woman out of her way as she slipped inside.

Rick jumped over the surprised purple humanoid on the floor and called out, "Excuse us. Sorry."

Eloise flipped a large switch as she passed through the opening of the first VR pod. A loud horn blasted a warning that the safety override for the VR tunnel had been deactivated.

"Hey, wait," Rick called as he hurried after her. "Are you sure you want to do that?"

He tried to turn the switch back to safety, but it wouldn't budge. She'd already gone inside. The override would remain until she exited and the next group turned it off. Rick didn't know what to expect inside the tunnel. Turning off the overrides meant the characters inside could touch, or grab, or do any number of things.

He thought of Viktor's words about the creatures.

He couldn't let Eloise face them alone.

Rick grabbed the VR door before it shut and went in.

Instantly a virtual program began to play. The metal construct disappeared to be replaced by a field of green and brown grass. The door closed behind him, disappearing from view and he knew this was meant to be a one-way trip. He was expected to walk forward into the VR world. A light flashed in his eyes as a computer scanned him, and an automated voice stated, "Humanoid unfiltered experience in progress."

The wind picked up, blowing against his clothes and undulating the landscape in tiny waves. The air smelled fresh, and the warmth of the sun beat down upon him from a bright blue sky. Clouds floated like torn pieces of material, worn and thin. He turned in a slow circle, letting the taller grasses brush his hands. Aside from the woman running away from him, there were no signs of other people.

"Eloise," Rick yelled, rushing after her.

Eloise kept moving across a field of grass toward the horizon. The veil fell from her hair and blew away. A holographic list appeared, running alongside him, citing the full solar benefits of the artificial sunlight and the carefully augmented sensory perceptions something-or-other. He swung his hand at it as if to push it out of the way, but the sales flyer merely rippled. A red triangle blinked on the scene, the only hint that there was an actual exit in the otherwise endless view.

A shout disturbed the serenity, and he glanced back to see five oversized thugs rushing into the field from the pavilion door. It slammed shut behind them, disappearing once more.

Rick caught up to Eloise as she touched the red triangle. Light shone as the entry to the next VR world appeared.

"Eloise," Rick said, trying to get her to turn around to see their pursuers.

"Stop calling me that. It's not my name," she answered.

"Easy enough, starbeam," Rick said, flashing her a smile.

She grabbed his arm and forced him into the light. A flash surrounded him as they stumbled onto a cobblestone road. The air quality changed, filling with the smell of baked meats and what could only be classified as sweaty bodies. Evening had come to the strange town as they left the sunlit field.

A narrow street led between towering buildings. Firelight shone from streetlamps. A man climbed a ladder to light them, appearing as if his only reason for being generated was to give light. Men with tall black hats escorted ladies down sidewalks. The gowns were shaped as if the women had backsides that protruded much farther than those of most humans. He'd be lying if he said he didn't want to lift the skirts and take a peek.

"I need to strip out of this damned fluffy dress," Not-Eloise grumbled.

Rick instantly turned his attention to her and

waited. Despite his better judgment, his body responded to the idea.

"Are you…?" She glanced down at his waist and arched a brow. "Seriously?"

Lacking any reason as to why he should be suddenly aroused while being chased through a VR tunnel by cyborgs, Rick winked at her to lighten the mood. "You're the one talking about undressing. I'm not usually into crowded, smelly streets, but hey, I'm willing to try anything once. Or twice."

To be fair, being chased by thugs wasn't exactly new territory for him. It happened often. Then again, judging by her annoyed expression, this wasn't new territory for her either.

Not-Eloise sighed heavily and pulled pins from her hair to uncoil the high locks even as she hurried down the streets.

"Hey, aren't you going to tell me what's going on?" he called before running to chase her. "Who's that Bucky guy and why is he sending men after us? Were those guys holding you hostage? Am I rescuing you from them right now?"

She didn't deign to answer as she searched the scene.

Massive beasts pulling carts neighed and whinnied as she charged through them to find a sidewalk. A woman in rags brushed past him, and he felt the coarseness of the material scratch the back of his hand.

The menu appeared again, this time reading, *"London Street Program. Building expansion packs available. Fully interactive games. Solve a serial killer mystery. Interview witnesses. Extensive lexicon. Catch the suspect before the killer finds you first."*

Great. Just great. He was horny, being chased by real world bio-jerks, and now running for his life from a programmed killer? Suddenly, being bored out of his mind on the ship was sounding better and better.

A woman appeared in an above window, glancing from behind tattered lace. Rick cut toward the building. "Come on, we can hide in here."

As he opened the door, he hit the program boundary. The entryway blurred and faded into a metal wall. A yellow box flashed, denoting the preview limits.

Not-Eloise appeared next to him and tugged his arm. "Keep moving."

"Easy, love, you act like five thugs are chasing us," Rick said.

"Five bionic thugs *are* chasing us," she answered.

"That was a joke," he said. "I know they're after us. I just don't know why. I'm still waiting for you to clue me in."

"It's not a joke if you have to explain you were joking," she rebutted.

"You're beautiful when you're scowling at me, Not-Eloise." Rick tried to caress her cheek, and she slapped his hand away in annoyance. "You know it's only a matter of time before you give in to the heat between us."

"Any heat you feel coming off me is anger," she quipped. "Everything was fine until your space cadet ass got in the way. Why can't you leave me alone?"

"We have unfinished business," Rick said.

"And what business is that?"

"Don't act like you didn't know there was something between us when we went to the mines."

"I could have killed you, but I didn't. The least you could do to repay me is stop forcing me into situations where I have to save you. Blast, you are infuriating!"

He followed her past the large animals pulling people in carriages. Someone screamed about having papers to sell. It was several moments before he could answer. "Wouldn't be one of the first times a woman bedded me in anger."

Not-Eloise stopped and turned to him. "What is wrong with you?"

Several of the generated characters paused and

looked toward them at the sound of her irritation. Rick ignored them.

"I'd imagine quite a lot, starbeam," Rick answered.

"Harper," she said.

"What?"

"My name is Harper Virant," she stated as if torn between being firm and completely exasperated.

Screams sounded behind them. Rick turned, not startled at first since it was a VR program. People began running down the sidewalk toward them, weaving through those characters whose programs hadn't triggered with fear. The animals became louder and bucked against their restraints.

"They're coming," Harper said. She grabbed a walking stick out of the hand of a passing man and swung it at the backside of one of the cart animals. The creature kicked up its legs and began running through the crowd.

"Excuse me, waif, what do you think you're doing?" the character demanded. The man grabbed Harper by the arm and tried to haul her toward him. With the safety overrides off for the tour, there was no filter to keep the man from hurting her.

Rick punched the man, causing him to stumble and let her go.

"Why did you turn off the safety?" he demanded.

She lifted the walking stick. "So I could find something to defend myself. I'm not about to face bionic mutants with my bare hands. The promoters won't let us die in here… I don't think."

They continued on, finally finding the triangle marking the exit on the side of a brick building. Harper pushed it, and they stepped through to the next display. The clank of metal floor grates marked their footsteps, and he hit Harper's back when she unexpectantly stopped.

"Blast it," she swore, eyeing her empty hand. The walking stick had disappeared, not transferring between scenes.

They were inside a passageway within a larger room. Glass cage walls lined both sides to keep them walking in a straight line. Each cage held a strange creature locked within a habitat with a button on the side that read, "Open."

Some of the creatures he recognized from Old Earth transmission waves he'd bootlegged, but others appeared as if caught from the darkest parts of the universe. The narrow space made the creatures feel too close for comfort, especially when they leaned against the glass.

Nameplates appeared next to the enclosures.

"*Wolfman,*" a humanoid monster covered with

fur stared from within a wooded habitat. The faintest glow of fire lit the distance. Yellowed eyes glowed as they followed Rick's movements. The man wore tattered clothing and howled a frighteningly hollow sound.

"*Swampy*," faced the wolfman from across the passageway. Draping vines over stagnant water surrounded him. It appeared as if this man had been made from the moss and pieces of organic debris floating around the murky water.

"*Clown Killer*," might have been the creepiest, with her painted face and ratty hair. The wide smile revealed sharp teeth stretching from ear to ear. The creature waved her hand slowly while holding brightly colored balloons that floated over her head. A knife laid on the trimmed grass near her feet as if it had been dropped in an effort to hide it.

"There's no weapon in here, at least none we can reach," Rick said. "Keep moving."

Rick threaded his arm through Harper's and led her away when she didn't step forward on her own. He felt her tremble.

"Do you smell that?" Harper asked.

Rick breathed deeply, detecting a slight musky odor. Harper reached for a dark habitat labeled, "*Vampire*," as if she would press the button to open it.

"Pheromones?" he guessed, seeing how her eyes

glassed over. The pale vampire's red eyes focused in on Harper and he parted his lips. Rick grimaced. "Oh, hell no. Get your own lady."

He grabbed Harper's arm and forcibly dragged her away, even as she stumbled and reached back.

"*Chimera. Fouke. Hydra. Vargr.*" The words meant very little to Rick and he didn't take the time to examine the creatures displayed.

"By all that is——" Harper gasped and tripped on her own feet as she passed a cage. A headless creature stared at them from large eyes in his chest.

"Don't look at them," Rick instructed, moving her past the "*Blemmyae*" enclosure.

They reached the end of the passageway and he glanced back.

He'd been wrong. There were plenty of weapons in here.

"Wait for me," he instructed, before hitting the triangle and shoving her through the doorway.

Rick hurried back toward the beginning of the display. The monsters appeared to have grown curious as they came even closer to the glass. Foggy breath misted the cage from within a snow-filled enclosure. The creature was pure white, even his eyes, and blended with his surroundings. His skin appeared formed of powder, with tiny flakes sluffing each time he moved.

"This might be the stupidest thing I've ever

done," Rick whispered to a headless woman carrying her own severed head by the hair.

His heart hammered in his chest and he tried to control the twitch of his muscles urging him to run. He lifted his hands toward Wolfman and Swampy's cages and let them hover. He stared at the door, waiting for the flash of light that would indicate the others were coming through.

Any second... Any second...

3

Harper's heart raced as Rick pushed her out of the monstrous zoo. She hated to admit that if he'd not been with her, she might have tried to free the mesmerizing creature. Or at least stared at the vampire like an idiot until Bucky's men found her. The sweet musk being pumped into the air had lured her, and it had felt very real. Of course, that was the point of Virtual Reality.

As her toe caught, she stumbled on a brick street. "Easy, Rick, I can—"

Her voice cut off when she turned and realized he wasn't with her. Brightly colored motorized vehicles moved toward a central building as a soft mist of rain fell. The red-orange roads matched the building facades. Unlike the London VR, this display was clean. Tree limbs drooped with fat white blossoms. Tall columns lined the buildings, rising two floors, though they appeared more for aesthetics than function.

Harper had trained in many VR environments and was well aware of the rules and limitations. The Nozando government wouldn't let anyone die in the displays, but safety override meant they could be injured enough to be taken to a medical booth. Some aliens were into that kind of thing and paid a lot of money for it.

She wasn't afraid of taking a beating, but there was no way she'd survive being stuck in the infirmary afterward. Not after betraying Bucky. He'd use members of his security team for parts to fix his bionic arms. And then he would tear her asunder.

"Rick?" She frowned. He hadn't come through the door with her.

Then it hit her what he'd mumbled when he pushed her. *"Wait for me."*

The characters in this VR scene wore strange clothes that didn't cover their limbs as if they expected a sun to shine through at any moment. The land crafts parked along the roadway in a variety of shapes and sizes were each fitted with rubber wheels that indicated they did not fly.

She lifted her hand and tried to find the doorway to the monster zoo. The VR had hidden the return route the second she'd come through, but if she could find the edge, she might be able to find her way back. When she stepped farther than she'd stumbled into the display, the VR world appeared to expand. She looked down. The ground didn't feel like it moved, but it was modified to keep her in the display.

"Dammit, Rick," she swore. He couldn't take on that many bionic guards.

Saving Rick from Bucky had been an impulse, much like the time she'd hit him over the head to keep him from being shot by an intergalactic cartel. Had she done nothing, Prince Bucky would have killed him. And the bionic jerk would have gotten away with it too. No one would fault a prince for murdering a smartass piece of space trash.

"Computer, where is the entry point?" Harper called into the crowd. Several of the characters looked at her and smiled.

"Can I help you, honey?" asked an older woman wearing bright red.

"How do I get out of here?" Harper asked.

The woman blinked as if her coding wasn't able to answer the question.

"Entryway. Starting point. Start," Harper said,

listing the words in hopes of triggering the program. There were probably instructions somewhere at the beginning of the VR display hall, but she'd run past the opening without checking. "Beginning!"

A light flashed, and a door appeared before her. She didn't think as she went through it.

"*Ba-a-a-a-lls!*" Rick yelled as he charged her. His arms were widespread, and she instantly lifted her hands in defense. Beeps sounded as he moved, and monsters were stepping into the passageway behind him. Their environments came with them, swamp and snow and forest, growing out of the enclosures to fill the hallway.

The smack of skin and metal flooded the area beneath the shrieks and growls. Her eyes widened. Bucky's guards were fighting the creatures.

"Run!" Rick ordered.

Killer Clown stepped from her cage holding a knife. Her eyes moved toward the brawl and then turned toward Rick's retreating back. She released the balloons and took a menacing step after Rick before disappearing.

The vampire's hands wrapped the edge of his cage, and it looked as if he pulled his floating body from the enclosure. He too followed Rick, gliding more than running, his arms outstretched.

"Rick, watch out," Harper warned, waving her

hand for him to hurry as if that would make him move faster.

As Rick neared her, the clown appeared between them, grinning her evil teeth-filled smile at Harper as she held her knife.

The vampire reached them, stretching his arm toward Harper across Rick and the clown as they collided in one big mass of bodies. He bared his fangs, eyes focused on her neck.

The clown stabbed the knife downward. Rick yelled, a primal sound. He slammed into the clown's back, grabbing her wrist to stop the blade from striking. He was almost too late as the tip of the knife sliced into Harper's shoulder.

It happened quickly. Harper let their weight push her back through the doorway. She fell toward the brick-laden ground of the clean town VR scene. The clown dissolved at the barrier. Rick's body flew toward Harper. There was no stopping his descent.

The vampire's hand disintegrated, and a second later she saw the creature staring at the door in what could only be angry disappointment before his face was replaced by the edge of the current world.

Rick tried to catch his weight, but the fall was awkward, and he ended up racking his manhood on her lifted knee. The force rammed her into the ground, and she cried out in pain.

"My balls," he groaned, rolling to the side as he cupped himself.

Harper drew her knees forward, trying to ease the pain in her lower back. They lay on the ground, cradling their injuries. Light rainfall misted them. Blood seeped from the knife wound. Too bad physical injuries didn't dissolve like the creatures had.

"It would seem I'm always saving you," Harper said as she pushed up from the ground.

"Or am I saving you?" Rick frowned, still cradling his manhood. "Those monster freaks should slow the cyborgs down.

"They prefer to be called bionics." Harper pushed to her feet and reached to help him up.

"My mistake. Wouldn't want to offend the jerkoffs," Rick quipped. He limped behind her as she moved down the sidewalk.

Storefronts were crowded along the walkway. Through windows, furniture, clothing, pottery, and other goods were displayed. Occasionally, one would smell like an experiment from the food simulators, not necessarily unpleasant, but definitely bizarre.

"If we get out of this alive, you need to stop following me whenever you see me," she said. Sure, he was attractive, and there was something about him that made her want to kiss and punch him at the same time, but Rick was a complication she couldn't afford. He'd already proven that more than once.

"We'll get out of this alive," he assured her. "And if you don't want me following you, sunbeam, maybe you should stop running away from me and admit what's between us."

"There is nothing between us."

"Are you denying the sexual tension that sparks each time you come near—"

"You don't know what you're messing with." She darted to the side as a dark green craft's tires rolled through a puddle to send a wave of dirty water in their direction.

"Why don't you tell me? How is it a drug trader with a fondness for black leather is suddenly disguised as some demure puritan from—where did you say you were from?"

"I didn't." It was bad enough she'd told him her real name. She wasn't about to give him any more personal information. Some memories didn't need to be resurrected.

The sales menu appeared. *"New Earth Settlement. Town Square. Western District. Choose from the following: Parade. 3471 Riot. Nightlife. Art Festival (Available Soon)."*

Rick started to lift his hand to select the nightlife option, and she slapped it down.

"No distractions. We need to find the exit," she said.

"I'm guessing it's straight ahead, behind that domed building with the road circling around it."

Another land craft rolled past as she lifted her hand to block the stream of water from hitting her. It might not be real, but she'd feel wet until they left this place.

"Selection made," a computerized voice said. "Enjoy."

"What did you do?" Harper demanded.

"Not me, sweet cheeks." Rick pointed toward her arm.

She lowered her hand, only to realize she'd bumped the menu when she'd tried to block the water.

Angry shouts sounded, and the sky darkened. The moisture disappeared. Fires lit the night, the orange glow casting over the forming crowd. The words "*3471 Riot*" blinked on the menu setting.

"*Power. Power. Power,*" a crowd chanted, each shout infused with rage.

"*Darkness. Dark. Dark,*" an opposing group responded.

Suddenly, a torch flew toward a building, breaking a window before setting it on fire. The act spurred an all-out brawl. The protestors turned on each other until it was impossible to reason who fought who or why. Regardless, it didn't take long for the hostility to find them. A wild punch landed on Rick's jaw and sent him sprawling. Someone jerked Harper by the arm, dragging her deeper into the throng. The rough movement jarred her already injured shoulder.

"Harper," Rick yelled, the sound faint beneath the rising voices.

Harper used everything she had to fight the thick press of humanoid bodies surrounding her. There wasn't enough room to maneuver properly, and her actions were limited by the mob of people.

"Computer, stop the riot," Harper yelled. "Stop the program. Show exit."

None of the commands worked.

She lost her footing and began a bumpy descent toward trampling feet.

"Harper!" Rick's yell proceeded his shadowed form diving over the heads of the crowd. He spread his limbs as he tumbled several people into a pile. The pressure was taken from Harper's body, and she was able to right herself. Rick struggled to his feet, only to grab her hand. He gave her a cocky grin. "Miss me?"

"Not even a little," she answered. She couldn't help returning the smile. Adrenaline pumped through her veins, and she loved the rush. He pulled her behind him as they escaped.

Rick used his shoulder to part the crowd, thrusting people aside. Harper tugged her hand free and punched a blond man wielding a brick. Together they ran along the edge of the throng toward the center building blocking the street.

"I see it," Rick said, altering their course. They hurried toward the glowing triangle. He pushed it and they leaped into the light. The angry shouts abruptly stopped when they passed through the door.

Panting hard, she placed her hand against a wall and took several deep breaths.

"Did they hurt you?" A soft, artificial green glow illuminated Rick's handsome features. She had to stop herself from grabbing hold of his face and kissing him. Harper remembered the arousing feel of his kiss, but he wouldn't remember hers.

"I'm fine," she answered at length.

"Try not to touch anything," he said.

"You try not to touch anything," she countered.

His eyes dipped to her bleeding shoulder.

"It's fine," she dismissed.

This VR world appeared to be an alien space station. A plastic-coated hallway gave them only one option for where to walk. The tube lights and rounded windows were fairly common.

Rick stopped at a window and peeked in. She

saw his mouth shift as he smiled. "I see a bed. Want to check it out?"

Harper arched a brow and leaned to look. The bed he referred to was a stasis pod in the style that had been popular centuries before advancements had been made in long-distance space travel. It was currently occupied by a half-dressed human female.

"I think they'll kick you out of the conference for sullying the reputations of the VR characters," Harper teased.

"Nonsense," Rick countered. "A night with me only enhances a reputation. You should try it and find out."

"Keep moving, lover boy," she laughed.

"I like you like this," Rick said.

"Compared to?"

"When you're tying me to a chair and threatening to kill me." Rick grinned. "Though, now that I think about it, the tying part isn't an issue."

"Keep walking." Harper pushed his shoulder. She glanced through the windows they passed, finding a laboratory filled with specimen tubes with brightly colored liquids, and what appeared to be a surgical unit. The silent, abandoned corridor frightened her more than the monster zoo.

A red light began to flash a warning, accompanied by a loud warning blast. One of the doors began to slide up.

"Nope." Rick pushed the triangle and they went through the next doorway.

They emerged inside a thick forest near a stone cabin. Smoke curled from the rooftop and a small garden was fenced along the front. A dirt path led through the trees, the ruts revealing that it was well-traveled.

"How long is this tunnel?" she grumbled. They had to be nearing the end.

Suddenly, Rick stopped.

"We need to keep moving," Harper said. "We have to be near the end of this thing. Once we're out, you should find your crew and get your ass into space. Bucky and his men will be looking for me. My wardrobe change won't throw them off for long. I'll make sure they don't follow you."

"Come with us," he said. "We can protect you."

"No." Harper wouldn't even consider it. That could never happen. "I'll be fine. I have my own ride off-world."

Rick held up his hand to her lips as if to warn her to silence. His head tilted, and he appeared concerned.

The warmth of his touch caused her to shiver. The memory of his kiss flooded her senses. There were things she wanted in her life that she could never have. She had made her choices and rarely regretted them. There was no future with Rick.

She pulled his fingers away, needing the intimate contact to stop, and whispered, "What do you hear? Is it that Wolfman again? This looks like his enclosure."

The forest reminded her of that hairy monster's display. She glanced at the cabin. The pieces of material covering the windows didn't move to indicate someone watched them. Except for the sound of birds, the woods were quiet.

Rick shook his head as he stared at her with a strange look on his face. His features had paled slightly and his lips moved, but no sound came out. She looked down to see if he was injured, unable to fathom what had spooked him.

She pushed past him and looked around, trying to see what he'd seen to make him stop. The forest reminded her of her childhood, but it wasn't anything special. There was an infinite number of such places scattered across the universes. She took a few steps, eyeing the treetops before leaning over to touch the leafy ground as she tried to see farther down the path. "What?"

"I…" He took a shaky breath. The sound of his feet shuffling on the dirt path behind her indicated he moved closer to her. "I think I love you."

Harper frowned and closed her eyes. Not again.

"We have a connection," he continued, the words soft and a little stunted. He touched her head, stroking the locks. "I feel it. It's tingling in my head. It's in my hands. What happened on the way to the mines? I know something happened. I feel possession, eagerness, like I know what is at the end of our kisses. I taste your... I feel it."

Harper took a deep breath. She reached beneath the hem of her skirt and ran her hand along her inner thigh.

"Can you feel...?" Rick appeared mystified by his own thoughts.

Finding what she was looking for, Harper pulled her last injector of Swipe from its holster. She twisted to look up at him as she bumped the tip into this thigh. The sting caused him to jerk his leg away. She wasn't prepared as his knee crashed into her back. She lost her balance and ended up squirting some of the medicine onto the ground. He quickly moved away from her.

"Wh—?" His eyes found her hand with the injector. "What did you do?"

"Don't worry about it. With luck you won't remember." Harper straightened, ready to catch him. She hoped that was true. At best the medicine erased short-term memory, and he hadn't received a full dose. It's why he remembered going to the mines, just not critical parts of that journey. He'd probably remember most of this VR tunnel too, just not his declaration of love for her. Even if he did start to remember their history, it would only come to him in broken fragments.

He blinked and took another step away from her. His foot tripped on a rut and he fell into a tree branch. A loud thud sounded as he knocked his head. The force sent him jarring backward, and she lurched behind him to stop his fall.

For all of her training, the inelegant transaction caused her to stumble more than catch. Rick's body landed against her seconds before they slammed to the ground. The breath shot from her lungs. For a stunned moment, she let him lie on top of her, his back against her chest, his dead weight pressing her down. She managed a gasp to draw air.

Harper pushed his arm and slid out from under him. Blood beaded his forehead where he'd struck the branch. She didn't mean for him to be injured.

"Blast it, Rick. You have to stop finding me. We can't keep doing this." She touched his cheek. If only he remembered their multiple times together like she did. He entered her thoughts more than she was willing to admit, especially late at night during those rare times she allowed herself to dream of what-ifs. Forgetting her was the best gift she could give him.

Without knowing how long the bionic thugs would be delayed, she didn't waste any time. She pulled Rick to sitting upright and then maneuvered him across the back of her shoulder to carry him. It wasn't the easiest of tasks, but one she'd practiced many times in VR training sequences. She hurried to the cabin, hoping the structure's programming allowed for a place to hide and wasn't just a digital-ized grid like the London building

Rick opened his eyes, vaguely aware of a dull ache in his head. He stood in a forest surrounded by trees. Somehow he knew which way to go and his feet took him in that direction, deeper into the woods, each trunk much like the next. There were no road signs, no real paths to follow beyond a few shuffled leaves littering the ground.

As if appearing out of nowhere, a small voice said, "They keep them imprisoned in stone."

Rick stopped and looked around. He heard a laugh, the kind of mischievous sound young girls made when they were playing. A ghost of movement caught the corner of his eye, and he thought he saw her for a second before she disappeared.

More from memory than sight, he knew she wore tunic pants and a loose shirt, and her hair was pulled back with a yellow ribbon.

"They keep them imprisoned in stone," she repeated, the words so far away he could barely hear them.

"I remember this place." Rick walked faster—over an incline, past the thorns, under a gnarled branch, through twin bushes, and then finally...

Rick stumbled as he came to a sharp drop-off. The cliff was practically obscured by trees, and it would have been easy to tumble over the side.

A wide mountain range spread before him. The view both stunning and heartbreaking at the same time.

This was home.

Well, one of them anyway.

"They keep them imprisoned in stone."

He knew that girl. She'd been a quirky little thing, but as tough as any kid he'd ever met. What was her name?

A small hand touched his arm, and he felt like he was again twelve years old. The nails were short and jagged as if she'd bit at them in worry or clawed her way through a mine shaft. His gaze followed her arm, the image of her blurry as if a memory was trying to come into focus.

"They keep them imprisoned in stone."

Sprout. He'd called her Sprout.

"Do you mean in a stone prison?" That was his part of this script. Sprout always had strange stories. Her face became clearer. He expected a smile, but her eyes were so sad, so worried.

"No. It said they turn them into stone." She held out her hands in front of her as if blocking an invisible blow and froze in the defensive position. Her lips barely moved as she said, "Actual statues."

"Why would they do that?" Rick looked up at the tree branches. The sound of the leaves was so distinct as if each one crashed in the wind and then paused.

"Someday I want to free them." Her voice became distant once more. "You should come with me. We'll free them together. Promise."

"It's just a story they tell," he dismissed. "There are no statue people."

Rick turned his attention back to her, but she was gone.

Actually, she'd been right. There *had* been statue people. His crew had found them.

"Sprout?" Rick called, still held firm in the virtual memory. How did the programmers know about this?

He turned from the cliff, searching for her. A sick feeling filled him.

"I found them, Sprout. I found the stone people.

They were prisoners on Florencia's Fifth Moon. We freed one—the only one there was to be freed," he called. "We were too late for the others. A warden destroyed most of the statutes before we found them so there was no one else to rescue.

Rick wanted her to know. She didn't answer.

He ran through the woods, but it only brought him back to the incline leading to the cliff. This world did not want him leaving this spot.

"Rick?"

He turned at the scared voice and froze. Sprout stood in the forest. Her eyes became the clearest yet, so dark and resigned.

He opened his mouth to ask what was wrong when a shot from a blaster pistol rang out.

Sprout's eyes widened, and she clutched her neck. Blood pooled between her fingers before spilling over. He tried to run to her, but her body dissipated as she fell. He reached after her, trying to bring her back.

A hard object struck his head, and he grunted. It took a moment for his eyesight to focus. The past was gone. He lay on his back under a wooden frame. Light came from both sides, partly obscured by a red woven blanket. What was he doing under a bed?

"She said to let you sleep."

"Sprout?" Rick tried to sit up at the sound of the young girl's voice, only to hit his head again.

"You shouldn't do that."

He looked for the source of the voice and found an upside-down face staring at him as if the girl hung over the side of the bed. Short red hair fanned from her face, framing the green of her reptilian eyes. A row of scales covered her forehead to her nose.

"She said to watch you. She said to bite anyone who tried to wake you." The child smiled, showing a hint of fangs in her mouth. "No one came."

"Move over, little starbeam," he said, reaching for the side of the bed to pull himself out from underneath.

The child sat on the bed in a silver leotard with a golden serpent embroidered up the side. The cabin home was tidy but sparse. A pungent smell came from the fireplace.

"Where are your parents?" He started to feel concern for her, only to remember she wasn't real. None of this was.

The child gave him a half-smile and glanced at the pot over the fireplace.

Her parents were in the…?

"All right then, little demon spawn." He patted her head. "I'll be going now."

With unexpected speed, the girl grabbed his hand and bit down. Tiny fangs pierced his flesh. The girl giggled as Rick snatched his hand away and ran for the front door.

"Ow, holy space balls, devil girl!" Rick swore as he cradled his injured hand. He glanced around for Harper, but she was nowhere to be found. If she'd stashed him in the cabin, she had most definitely headed on without him.

Rick ran through the trees, over the rutted path, as he looked for the exit. This horrible VR adventure hall better be over soon. He glanced back to make sure the serpentine humanoid wasn't running after him.

He shook his hand as if to fling off the pain. Blast it all, that bite stung.

His head ached. His back was sore. His stomach felt like it had been punched.

What the hell had happened? How had he ended up under a bed?

"She said to let you sleep."

Harper. Harper had left him with the girl.

They were being chased by bionic men.

They'd passed a monstrous zoo, a city riot, a forest. He looked around. Apparently, he'd never left the forest.

The dream from his childhood tried to unfurl

inside him, whispering its forgotten secrets. He ignored it. Now was not the time.

A screech sounded, and he looked back. He heard the devil child but couldn't see her.

Though the woods looked vast, there wasn't anywhere for Harper to go but toward the exit. He heard the steady crunch of leaves behind him as footfalls chased him. The screeching became louder. The triangle emerged, and he ran as fast as he could toward it.

"*Reeeee-ah-ah-ah,*" came the child's cry.

Rick turned in time to see her lunging for him. He tried to leap toward the exit. His foot caught on something, and instead he fell through the door as the child reached for him.

A light flashed, and he saw Dev stepping out of his path as Rick fell to the ground.

Rick landed on concrete and slid. A crowd laughed. He jerked to a stop as Jackson grabbed his ankle only to instantly let go. It appeared as if his two friends had been waiting for him to emerge.

People had gathered to watch the exit, entertained as terrified guests came out.

Breathless and more than a little beat up, Rick grinned. "Thanks for the assist, fellas."

Dev arched a brow. "We haven't been here a full day and you're already causing mischief."

"No, I—" he tried to protest. "I found the woman."

Dev and Jackson both looked at the VR exit before sharing an amused look.

"Figures that even virtual women want to hurt you." Jackson offered a hand to help him up.

Dev remained standing with his arms crossed.

"No, I found the woman. Harper," Rick insisted as he was hefted to his feet. They were in a conference room lined with chairs around the center stage where they now stood. Groups of people had assembled in clusters around the auditorium. Now that he stood in one place, he felt as if he floated in water. His vision blurred slightly, and he rubbed his eyes. "The woman."

"Yeah, we know." Jackson released his hand only to grab him by the elbow to escort him off the stage into the aisle. A few aliens blocked their path.

Rick searched for Harper in the crowd.

"Security," Jackson said in an authoritative tone. "Step aside. Coming through. Dangerous lunatic has been apprehended. Step aside. Clear a path."

"Hey, now, wait," Rick protested.

Dev gave him a small shove in the back to shut him up.

Jackson pointed upward. A monitor showed the inside of the VR tunnels, flipping through scenes like a security monitor. People stood in the endless field, appearing annoyed as a security officer blocked their exit to the London exhibit. Yet another group stood in London, appearing to have fun exploring, even as they too were barred from exiting. They stood in the middle of the road as holographic animals walked through them.

A medic team was in the monstrous zoo VR program giving medical attention to the bionic thugs who'd been disabled by the displays. Janitor droids cleaned the biological fluids that had dripped from their broken tubing. The monsters were all back in their cages and not looking happy about it. Whoever had programmed them surely had some psychological issues to work out.

Another clean-up crew worked on the riot scene, moving through the displayed characters as if they were no more than ghosts. It looked like a bionic guard had made it that far before being overtaken by the angry mob.

And finally, the forest was empty except for the serpentine child sitting on her bed, smiling sweetly so that her little fangs showed.

A small shiver worked over Rick. He glanced down at his hand, still seeing the bite marks.

Jackson gave a small laugh. "Rick's scared of a girl child."

"Hey, she's not some innocent little starbeam.

That thing ate her parents," Rick defended. He held up his hand. "She tried to eat *me*."

There was no sign of Harper in the VR. Hopefully, that meant she'd escaped.

The walkway became congested as they left the auditorium and entered the pavilion. Jackson navigated the crowd, weaving through at a clipped pace. Rick tried to pull free of the man's grasp.

"Slow down. I have to find Harper," he said. "We can't leave her."

"We don't have time for your imaginary love affairs," Jackson said. "We need to leave. We're meeting everyone on the ship."

To his surprise, it was Dev who stopped Jackson's progress. "Who is Harper? Is that what you're calling the queenpin now?"

Rick nodded. "Did you see her?"

"Yes." Dev turned his head sharply, his eyes focusing on something Rick could not see before he motioned at Jackson to continue walking. "Pavilion security is on their way."

"Come on, fly boy," Jackson said. "Violette is preparing the ship for takeoff."

Rick couldn't help the small wave of possessiveness he felt at the thought of another pilot in his cockpit. He had very little that he could call his own and being pilot of his ship was one of them. Ever since the first time he'd sat behind a flight panel, he'd understood what it meant. Flying was freedom. It was escape. It meant never having to go back.

Rick could forget his past. He was good at forgetting. He shoved those memories into their painful little trap and never let them out. In fact, they'd been buried for so long they'd rotted into unrecognizable scraps.

He automatically smiled as they passed the fur-headed females he'd seen upon arrival. His gaze darted past them. He needed to find Harper.

"Which way did she go?" Rick asked Dev. When the man didn't answer, he said louder, "Dev, you said you saw her. Where did she go?"

Instead of answering, Dev grabbed his free arm and helped Jackson walk him toward the docking lot. "Three on the left."

"Two on the right," Jackson answered.

"One in the middle." Rick mocked their serious tone.

"Why are we saving him again?" Jackson asked.

"Captain's orders," Dev answered.

"Fine, I get it." Rick shook his arms to loosen their hold. "You can't live without me. Now let me go."

"Hey, you, stop! What's your authorization code?"

The shout caused both Dev and Jackson to walk

faster, dragging him with them. They didn't turn to see who yelled.

"Halt!"

Rick was no match for a Bevlon and a super soldier. The men lifted him by his arms and began to run in tandem. He tried to move his legs, but his feet dangled over the ground. They dropped him long enough to maneuver through the large sliding door leading to the docks. Seconds later, they had him back in the air as they sprinted past a long line of ships. They turned a corner, letting his feet bounce on the floor before lifting him once more.

"Let me down," Rick protested, kicking his legs. He tapped the back of Jackson's knee, forcing it to bend. When the man stumbled and released him, Rick began running on his own. Dev was forced to let go.

The sound of footfall followed them, propelling him on. Rick would be lying if he said he didn't like being chased. Danger made him feel alive.

Lochlann stood next to the wide cargo loading plank waving his arm for them to hurry. The purr of the ship's engine sounded in a low hum to welcome him home.

"Coming in hot," Dev called.

Lochlann led the way up the docking plank and hovered his hand over the door lock.

Lucien appeared near the top of the plank to

look. He scratched the back of his head. "You call that hot? She's just a little slip of a thing."

Raisa joined Lucien, leaning over to peek out as her husband rushed forward. "Rick, what did you do this time? She looks like she means business."

Rick made it to the metal docking plank before glancing back. Judging by the shouts and footfall, he'd expected to see two or three guards on their tail.

Instead, he found Harper. She wore a tight shirt and matching crimson pants. Apparently, she'd had time to change her clothing after abandoning him with the snake girl.

"Let's move," Lochlann ordered, hitting the button. The plank began to rise beneath him, carrying him up into the ship.

"No, wait!" Rick's eyes met Harper's, knowing what she was going to do.

"I said let's move," Lochlann commanded.

"Harper, don't," Rick yelled. "Lochlann stop the—"

Harper dove forward into the narrowing opening only to slide across the metal grate. It barely missed clipping her foot. The door would have taken it off easily. The metal sealed shut.

Dev grabbed two weapons from the cargo hold wall and tossed one to Jackson, who shoved his wife behind his back. Raisa didn't protest as he used his body to shield her.

"Don't move," Dev ordered, pointing his weapon at Harper.

"Easy," Rick said. "She's with me."

"Even more reason," Jackson said. "Raisa, love, get out of the cargo hold, please."

She didn't leave.

"Is that…? Holy space balls, the queenpin's back? Captain, open the hatch so Dev can throw her dangerous ass out," Lucien said, waving his hands. "Throw her out. Throw her out!"

"No—" Rick tried to protest.

"Miss me?" Harper smiled at Lucien even as she tried to catch her breath. The look was taunting and probably not the smartest, considering she'd just stowed away on their ship. She lifted her hands in surrender toward Dev as she sat up and winced a little. From his position, Rick detected her bloody knuckles.

The ship lurched as Violette engaged the engines for takeoff.

"Too late," Harper said.

"Says who," Dev answered. "Give us one reason why we shouldn't just eject you into the deep black?"

Harper glanced at Rick. He had to admit he was curious as to her answer. She had left him behind after all, in the clutches of the bitey demon spawn.

"I saved his life." Harper gave a small nod in his direction.

"Nice try. I saved *your* life," Rick disagreed.

The ship rocked, and they all stumbled and slid to the left. Harper grabbed on to a cargo strap and held tight to keep from sliding as she stayed on the floor.

Rick fell into a metal crate, smacking his sore hand in the process. "Blast it, Vi! What are you doing to my baby?"

Lochlann and Dev spread their arms as they were forced to balance their footing. Jackson placed a hand on the wall and leaned into it while holding on to Raisa's waist with his gun hand, no longer aiming at Harper. His eyes never wavered from the intruder.

Rick relaxed as they stopped pointing the weapons at her. They might threaten, but they wouldn't kill her. He pushed up as soon as the ship righted itself and ran past Dev out of the cargo hold. He hurried toward the cockpit, intent on taking over, only to stop and return to the cargo area.

"Don't toss her out," he yelled at the others before leaving once more, only to stop and return a second time. "And don't put Lucien or Viktor in charge of—"

Violette's flying took them sharply to the right. Rick stumbled the wrong direction down the passageway. If he didn't take over the controls soon, Violette was liable to steer the ship straight into a star.

As he ran past the cargo door, he yelled, "Don't do anything. I'll be back!"

5

Harper was used to people hating her. The eyes of Rick's crew stared down at her like they expected her to attack. Joke was on them. Various parts of her body throbbed in pain—the cut from the killer clown, her midsection from an unfortunate series of blows, and now her knuckles from the metal of the loading plank. By the sting in her side, she would guess she'd broken a rib or two. Until she found a handheld medic, she wouldn't be fighting anyone—let alone a Bevlon warrior and his fellow pirates.

She was also used to people loving her—not the real her, but the her she allowed them to see. It was her job to play a part. What she wasn't used to was Rick. He wasn't like the other men she'd met. He wasn't a job. In fact, he was quite the opposite. He was a damned inconvenience.

Harper should feel bad about taking his memories, but she didn't. It was for the best if he forgot certain things, including her. It would take more than a jab from her injector to erase everything, but accessing the kind of specialized equipment she'd need to erase herself completely from his memories would require bringing him home. Her bosses would find it easier, and more cost effective, to kill a space pirate rather than rehabilitate him since pirates by nature were untrustworthy criminals. So, thigh jabs it was.

Damn. She was out of Swipe injectors. Bucky was so boring she might have jabbed him a few times extra just to get him to leave her alone.

The ride smoothed and she let go of the cargo strap. She lifted her hands but kept her arms close to her sides. "How's it been, fellas?"

A woman attempted to come forward from beside Jackson. "I'm Raisa. We haven't—"

Jackson stepped to the side to block her advance. "What are you doing here?"

"I need a ride." Harper began to stand, only to think better of it as Dev and Jackson stepped forward. "Figured I'd hitch one from old friends."

"We are not friends," Dev said. "You can stay in the prison hold."

"I could," she agreed with a glance at Lucien, "but I'll just escape again."

Lucien furrowed his brow but didn't respond.

Bloody novas, her side hurt. Sliding onto the ship had been a necessary, if not a stupid idea. If she'd thought appealing to their better natures would work on this crew, she'd beg to use their medical booth. Instead, she tried to keep her breathing steady. Men like this respected toughness in others.

"What happened to you?" Raisa's head poked out from behind Jackson's back. "Who are you running from?"

Harper gave a small laugh. "That would be a long list."

Let them think she was a criminal.

"Well," the woman answered. "We can't fault her for that. I mean, we're not exactly a ship full of fare-thee-wells."

"You're speaking gibberish. Have you been talking to Rick again?" Jackson frowned as he turned to glance at Raisa.

"What does that even mean?" Dev asked.

"Fare-thee-wells were a sect of devout Earthlings who tried to live the divine and convert alien worlds when Old Earth humans began space travel," Harper said. "They never stayed long in one place."

"See, it's a real thing." Raisa shrugged. "I like talking to Rick. He makes me laugh, and he'll try any food I put in front of him."

"That green slime sludge was not food," Lucien stated, as if continuing an old argument.

"Maybe we can discuss the ship's culinary menu later," Dev said.

"Agreed," Jackson said. "Lucien, take my wife out of here please."

"Come on, Raisa." Lucien took the woman's arm. "Let's go make something gross and see if Rick will eat it."

"You're not going to let them hurt her, are you?" Raisa asked Jackson. "I don't know what she's done, but she needs help now."

Harper deepened her breathing, testing her lungs as she filled them to capacity. Even though it hurt, she was moving air in and out. She'd broken her ribs before, but this pain somehow felt different.

Jackson's eyes met Harper's, and he answered, "Not unless she makes us."

Raisa started for the door, only to stop and frown. "Are you... injured?"

Harper shook her head in denial but touched her side. Her fingers found a small protrusion beneath her shirt.

"She's bleeding. We need to get her to the medical booth." Raisa pointed at Harper's waist.

Harper glanced to her hand. Blood stained her fingertips where she'd bled through her shirt. A sharp jab hit her side, even though she didn't touch it again. She grunted and held her breath.

Raisa started for her. Dev grabbed her arm. "Careful, she's more dangerous than she seems."

"Help her, or I will," Raisa demanded.

Captain Lochlann had been eyeing her quietly. She couldn't tell what he was thinking, though she did see a strange yellow glow flash through his gaze. He didn't move. "Dev, check her."

Dev stepped closer and peered down at Harper.

"Hi there, big guy," Harper said, not moving from her place on the metal floor.

"Where is the blood coming from?" Dev asked.

"My body," Harper said.

"Do you require a medical booth?" Dev questioned.

"Honestly, I'd prefer a handheld if you have it." She knew way too much about the Medical Alliance for Planetary Health to trust any medical booth equipment they made straight off the assembly line. All her personal records and DNA makeup would be sent to the main facility. It was a little something the MAPH didn't like to include with the sales pitch.

"As you wish. Stand up. We're taking you to the prison hold." Dev motioned for her to stand.

"Wait, what?" Raisa protested.

Harper tried to stand, but her legs were weak and she was forced to grab the cargo strap to pull her weight.

At Jackson's look, Lucien threaded his arm through Raisa's and pulled her from the cargo area. "Come on, Raisa. We shouldn't be here."

Harper leaned into the crate. The ship vibrated violently before a loud metal clank sounded. None of the remaining men appeared concerned, so she ignored it.

The protrusion beneath her fingers felt cylindrical. She frowned and finally lifted her shirt to look at it. A metal disc had adhered to her flesh.

"That son of a comet-sucking whore side stitched me," Harper swore. She pulled at the disc, trying to pluck it from her flesh. Her finger slid over the bloody metal.

"What is a side stitch?" Lochlann asked, leaning to get a closer look. Red lights flashed in a pattern as they appeared to race around the circular device.

"It's an Ingeniarian tracker," she said, digging her fingers around it and pulling, to no avail. "And I need to get it off before it fuses to my bone."

"I thought you said the pavilion guards were after Rick for disrupting their adventure tunnel," Lochlann said.

"They were chasing us, and then they weren't.

This one appeared in their place," Dev answered. "She must have taken out the guards."

"The pavilion guards did that to you?" Jackson asked.

"The guards?" She scoffed. "Those two-bit hacks? They'll wake up with headaches later. No, the bionic black hole Prince Bucky's security team did this to me..." Harper muttered as she kept trying to pull it.

"Who's Prince Bucky?" Jackson asked.

"He's, um, kind of my betrothed," Harper answered. The device didn't budge. She wrapped the cargo strap around a wrist and held on to it with both hands as she took a deep breath. She glanced at Dev. "I need you to pull this thing out of me. Hard and fast."

She'd picked him out of the three because he was obviously at least half-Bevlon, and those aliens weren't squeamish when it came to pain.

"Perhaps the medical booth would be best," he answered.

Harper frowned. Perfect. She'd found the only Bevlon who didn't enjoy inflicting harm.

"I'll do it." Jackson stepped forward and lifted her shirt. He didn't hesitate as he formed a claw around the side stitch, dug his fingers in, and pulled.

Harper's legs gave out, and she screamed as it felt like her entire rib cage was being yanked from her flesh with pliers. Her hold on the strap was the only thing that kept her upright.

"Stop," Lochlann ordered.

Jackson instantly obeyed. Her side throbbed, and she felt a hot tear roll down her cheek.

"That's not working," Lochlann said. She glanced over at the captain. His expression pulled tight in distaste. "Put her in the medical booth."

"No," Harper managed, righting her shaky legs. "These little bastards are still new. I don't know how they will react to a scan like that. It could be better for the ship if we shoot it off."

"That could cause a reaction as well," Dev denied.

"Yeah, but look at it this way, if it does, you'll be rid of me," Harper answered. She hated the idea of being tracked more than she feared death. After being near the brink as many times as she had, the black void of an afterlife was about as welcoming as a well-deserved nap.

"Hey, what's going on back there?" Rick's voice came over the intercom. "I heard a scream."

"Get Viktor," Lochlann said, ignoring Rick. "Maybe he can take it apart."

"I'll go." Jackson left the cargo hold.

The unit on her side dug itself deeper, and she bit back a moan as she felt it moving.

"Captain?" Rick's voice demanded.

Harper took a deep breath, and said, "I don't mean to be an ungrateful guest, but could we hurry this along? The guy who ordered this done isn't going to be happy with me, or the people who took me. Before the Bevlon——"

"Blast it all," Rick insisted over her words. They all ignored him. "Captain? What's happening?"

"——suggests tossing me into the deep black, you should know that probably won't keep Bucky's men from tracking you. And I know what you're thinking, but if you try to give me to him it won't go well. He has a helluva temper. All those bionic juices have flowed to his brain." Harper flinched and pressed her hand beneath the device as if that could stop the pain.

"She will not be standing much longer," Dev noted. "We should take her to Viktor."

Lochlann nodded. "Do it."

Dev came for her and Harper automatically stiffened in defense. His brow arched in warning before he dipped down and slipped his arms behind her knees and back. He lifted her easily. His body cast off so much heat that he bordered on fiery.

Harper kept hold of the strap. She was too weak from pain to fight him properly, but her hand refused to let go. He took a few steps before being forced to stop. Her arm stretched wide as the strap became taut.

"Drop it, or I drop you," Dev warned.

Harper unclenched her hand.

Dev walked her toward the doorway. The strap unwound itself from her wrist and fell away. The jarring vibration of each footstep caused small gasps to exit her lungs. She closed her eyes tight, even as her brain told her she needed to pay attention to where they took her.

Harper forced herself to concentrate. She looked at the passageway, eyed the metal doors, and noted the random scratches and marks in the surfaces. Each would serve as a landmark to help her find her way around.

"If someone doesn't answer me, I'm going to stop flying the ship," Rick's intercom voice blasted.

"Rick, shut your black hole." Lochlann's voice followed them as he stayed behind to answer the pilot. His words did not blast over the intercom, indicating he used a private comm line. "No one is killing your drug peddler. We're debugging her. Just fly the ship and watch our tail. Find my wife and tell her to meet me in the commons. I need to talk to her."

"Alexis, your husband is looking for you," Rick's voice announced. "Get to the commons."

"I can walk," Harper protested, stiffening in Dev's arms to get him to put her down. He kept going.

"What has Rick got us into now?" Viktor appeared in the corridor. Jackson was behind him. His red-green eyes glanced over her before recognition dawned in his expression. "Oh, no, not her again."

"Captain needs you to disarm her," Dev said.

Jackson lifted a canvas bag. The contents clanked. "I have his tools."

Dev turned into a small room and dropped more than placed her on a cot. Looking at Viktor, he motioned for him to get started.

"I'm not sure I want to," Viktor muttered. "She scares me."

Jackson gave him a small shove into the room. "Stop goofing around. Can you deactivate it or not?"

Harper gave Viktor a weak smile and winked. "Been a long time. It's Viktor, right?"

"Yeah." Viktor looked her over. "So what exactly am I deactivating?"

Harper reached for her shirt and lifted. "Side stitch."

"You ever heard of these?" Dev asked.

Viktor flicked his finger against the device before pulling back fast. "Is it some kind of explosive?"

"I hope not," Harper said. "Tracker."

"The tech looks familiar." Viktor ran his finger around the perimeter.

"It's from the factories on Ingeniare," she said.

Viktor instantly let go and lifted his hands up and back. "You're telling me this is an Ingeniarian tracker?"

Harper nodded. "Yeah, so if you don't mind, would you get it out of me before it integrates further? I don't think my dresses will fit right with this thing hiding underneath and I would like to date again."

"This is unsettling. Do you notice how she's almost like she's a female Rick?" Jackson muttered to Dev. It didn't appear to be a compliment.

"Ah...?" Viktor let loose a long sigh and did not sound confident. "Maybe we should ask Raisa? If she can sense—"

"No," Jackson stated flatly.

"Why not Raisa?" Harper asked. "If she knows how to—"

"She doesn't," Jackson said, his tone allowing no further discussion on the matter of his wife.

Viktor reached his hand toward Jackson. "Laser."

Instead of digging in the canvas sack, Jackson set it on the floor and gently turned it over so the tools slid out into a pile. Harper's eyes automatically went to a metal cutting blade.

"This party is going to suck," she muttered as

she lowered onto the cot while keeping the side stitch exposed.

"What are you going to do?" Jackson asked.

"Does it look like it has explosives?" Dev added.

"What range if—" Jackson tried.

"I need you to step out and stop asking me questions," Viktor commanded, his words a little shaky. "I'm not touching the body of the device. I'm going to try to cut the claws where it is attached."

Harper glanced toward the men in time to see them moving to stand in the corridor. They stayed within eyesight of her.

"This is almost guaranteed to hurt," he said. Then to the guys behind him, he added, "Did Alexis fix the handheld medic yet? We need painkillers, rum, anything."

Harper grabbed his hand. "We need to do this. I can feel it digging. I'll be fine. Just don't stop once you start."

With any luck, she'd pass out.

"I'll try not to burn you with the laser," he whispered.

Currently, that was the least of her worries.

"Don't stop," she ordered, closing her eyes. She grabbed the edge of the cot and braced herself for the pain to come.

The hum of the laser caught her full attention. Viktor placed a hand on her side. Heat radiated as it neared her flesh. She clenched her teeth in antic-ipation.

Suddenly, the ship jerked and she rolled forward.

"Blasted," Viktor swore, his voice tinged with panic. "Tell Rick or Vi or whoever is flying to keep us steady."

Harper took a hard breath and stared into the man's red-green gaze. "Can you do this or not?"

He nodded.

"Then do it," she ordered. "Now."

Harper again braced herself. She concentrated on keeping her breathing even. The hum neared her. The heat hit her flesh. She gripped the cot as tight as she could, determined to hold still. Sweat beaded her brow.

Don't move. Don't move. Don't blasting move.

The laser hit metal, *zzzz*.

Pain radiated from her side, and she opened her mouth wide in a silent cry. She knew it would only get worse.

"Stop!" came a feminine cry.

"*Agh*," Viktor yelled, jumping back. "Don't scare me like that. Alexis, what are you doing in here?"

"Give me the laser, I'll do it." Harper pushed up from the cot in irritation. For space pirates, these were an indecisive lot.

"Don't do that," Alexis answered. "The temper-ature of the laser isn't hot enough to effectively cut the metal used by the Ingeniarians in their bionic factories."

Harper eyed the woman and frowned. Her face was all too familiar. It had been broadcasted in every fueling dock. "Alexis? The captain's wife?"

Viktor nodded.

"The captain is married to a robot?" Harper couldn't help the slight exasperation in her voice. The Alexis model droid was a companion unit for lonely men who would rather sleep with silicone than make an effort with a woman who did not require programming. Harper would be less judgmental of it if they made as many male versions for the ladies.

"Yes," the three men answered in unison. Lochlann appeared in the doorway as if he'd been running.

"Yes, I am the Alexis Companion model nine-point-seven. I prefer the term pleasure droid," Alexis said. Her eyes slowly changed from brown to blue.

"I'm sure you do, sweetheart," Harper muttered. The ship vibrated, angering Harper's already frayed nerves. "Can we usher the walking food simulator out of here and get on with this?"

Alexis turned around and began to mumble to herself.

Great. She'd hurt the robot's feelings.

"Dev, join Rick and your wife in the cockpit. Tell them what's happening and make sure no one is following us. Be sure to scan all the frequencies," Lochlann ordered.

Dev nodded and left.

"Jackson, go to Raisa and Lucien. Catch them up," Lochlann added.

Harper noted that the captain sent the men to be with their wives. She wondered if there was something they weren't telling her, and then instantly assumed there would be a lot they wouldn't tell her.

"Give me the laser," Harper insisted. This was taking too long. "I'll do it myself."

Alexis turned back around. Her eyes were slightly glazed over but were clearing. "You have to remove the top of the disc and expose the insides to make the claw retract. Hand it to me. I have the steadiest hand."

Harper's palm was still extended toward Viktor as he retrieved the laser from the floor. To her surprise, he handed it to the droid instead. Harper would have protested but her side throbbed and she just wanted the damned tracker out of her. As she lay back down, she mumbled, "You better not be programmed to be all emotional and squeamish."

"Trust me, sweetheart," the robot said, mocking

Harper's earlier insulting tone, "I'm anything but squeamish."

Alexis placed her hand firmly on Harper's side, and the hum of the laser sounded. The droid's eyes had turned to a deep brown. Harper braced herself as Alexis drew the laser parallel to her skin to cut around the perimeter of the disc. The vibrations hurt insomuch as it jarred the side stitch, but not nearly as bad as Viktor's plan. A tiny trail of smoke drifted from where the robot worked.

Harper tried to look, but Alexis pushed down harder. "Don't move. I don't want to nick the power source."

The ship vibrated, but the motion didn't faze the droid who stayed focused on her task.

Harper took back all her previous thoughts about the bimbo units.

Yay for pleasure droids!

"Almost there," Alexis muttered before the hum of the laser stopped. Her hold eased up, and she handed the laser to Viktor.

"Well done, my love," Lochlann said.

Alexis pulled the lid from the side stitch and gave that to Viktor as well. She looked at the floor before finding a metal pick with a sharpened tip. Rust had begun to form at the base where the handle met metal.

"I can promise this is going to sting," Alexis said,

not pausing to give Harper time to brace herself as she pushed the tip into the exposed side stitch.

"Ow, holy space balls," Harper cried out as the unit pressed down. She felt movement inside her body as if the tips of the claws broke off her rib. They pulled out.

Alexis plucked the unit off her side.

Harper moaned and covered the wound with her hand, thankful that the side stitch was gone. "Oh, thank you, Alexis model whatever you said. I promise never to make fun of your kind again."

"Let's see what's inside this thing," Alexis mused as she tipped the bottom half of the tracker over into her palm. A glowing power unit slid onto her hand, and she instantly stiffened and fell back. Her eyes flashed wildly with colors, and she appeared as if she was having a seizure.

"Alexis?" Lochlann called out in panic as he went to his robot wife.

Harper sat up slowly, more curious about the robot that helped her than worried. It wasn't alive, after all. Machines could be repaired.

Alexis began to mutter even as the tremors continued. "Space travel holo-brochure. Planet of Ingeniare. Head of the Ingeniare Alliance consisting of three highly important technology factory planets. Ruled by a large royal family whose sole mission has been to give work to those under their command. Irrelevant to the situation. Reexamine."

"What in the black holes is wrong with her?" Harper asked, staring at the shaky droid spewing information.

"Alexis, relevant," Lochlann stated loudly, patting her face. "Relevant."

Viktor joined him on the ground and began trying to pry open her fist holding the power source.

"Scientific opinion paper. Obscure. The unspoken dangers of the Ingeniarians bionic factories by E'on Trek. Deceased. Poor working conditions by an enslaved population on the third planet of the Ingeniare Trio are not worth the technological gain to the known universes. Relevant to the situation. Ingeniare Trio. Home to the power—"

"Alexis, stop," Lochlann ordered.

The droid kept going. "—manufacturing plant. Off-limits to visitors. Life span of the Ingeniare Three population is halved from those on the other two planets."

Harper glanced at her side. Blood seeped through her fingers from the deep wound. The men kneeling on the floor hardly appeared concerned with her. She pulled her shirt tight around her waist, trying to put pressure on the wound as she tucked the edges. It helped some. A bandage would have been better. A handheld medical unit would have been better than that.

"Petty criminals and political uprisers are often transported to the inhumane, in-alien-mane living conditions," Alexis continued. "Work hours consist of three-quarters of every day."

"How does she know that?" Harper demanded. That information wasn't public knowledge. The Ingeniarian royals worked hard to maintain a friendly image.

"We need to get this thing out of her hand," Viktor said. "I'll have to break her fingers."

"Relevant to the situation. Classified file number 7890-8889. Ingeniarian top-secret protocol alpha four. Infiltration team to undermine the power of the royal family..."

Lochlann took over, pulling at the droid's pinky finger so hard it cracked. He shook her hand violently, forcing the power disc to fall to the floor.

"...to undermine the—" Alexis gasped sharply and sat up. She took several deep breaths.

Lochlann cradled the hand he'd injured. "I'm so sorry, my love."

The droid trembled. "The nanoids will repair it. Thank you for getting that thing off me."

Harper frowned. "How did she know that?

They ignored her.

"What happened?" Viktor asked. He picked

the power source up from the floor and dropped it into the shell of the broken side stitch. He shook out the insides from the other half of the unit and pressed it to the top to form a protective case, which he then held pinched between two fingers.

"It reactivated the…" Alexis glanced in her direction. "My connection."

"You mean…?" Lochlann helped Alexis to her feet.

She nodded. "Yeah."

Harper tried to decipher what they were not telling her. She swayed on the cot, feeling dizzy. She couldn't be sure if it was the ship that rocked or her balance.

"Put that power source in the safe," Lochlann ordered. "Keep it away from Alexis."

Viktor nodded.

"How did she…?" Harper's words trailed off when Alexis' gaze met hers.

"I need to talk to you, *now*," Alexis told Lochlann. "Viktor, go get Dev to keep an eye on her."

"Shouldn't we do something about her side first?" Viktor asked. "She doesn't look well."

"Get Dev," Alexis said. Viktor hurried from the small room.

Harper wondered why they would be taking

orders from a droid. None of this made sense. Who *were* these pirates?

Alexis pushed her husband toward the door. "We'll bring you supplies for your side soon." They passed through the threshold. "Until then…" She placed her hand on a sensor, and the door slid shut. Harper heard the telltale slide of industrial locks. She glanced up. There was no grate access to the ceiling. In her current state, she wouldn't be escaping anytime soon.

That blasted droid's expression had been too knowing. The only question was, how much did she know, and how did she know it? Programming glitch? Surely Alexis couldn't know the truth, even with the classified information she'd had access too. She probably thought Harper was an escaped criminal from Ingeniare Three.

Yes. That had to be it. That was the most logical assumption.

Harper lay down on the cot and took a deep breath. She turned so that she could keep an eye on the door and the wound side faced upward toward the ceiling. Rest sounded good about right now.

6

"Your girlfriend is HIA," Alexis stated, her eyes focused on Rick.

He'd thought they were taking him to see Harper, but instead they had tried to sit him down in the common area. The ship was on autopilot, but Violette was in the cockpit monitoring. So far there were no signs they were being followed.

Rick gave a small laugh. There was no way Harper worked for the Human Intelligence Agency. He made a move to leave. "Yeah, right. Now tell me what's going on with Harper. I want to see her. Dev said she had something stuck in her side. Is that what that screaming was about?"

Rick knew no one on the crew would hurt a woman unless they were left with no choice.

"Rick, we need to talk about this," Lochlann

stated firmly. He stood beside his wife as they blocked his path. "She's a threat."

His expression fell. "Did she say she was HIA?"

Alexis glanced at Lochlann.

"Did she say the words?" Rick insisted.

Alexis shook her head in denial. "No. I accessed some files. They're still jumbled, but I'll sort them out soon."

"Then we don't know for sure," Rick said. Though Alexis was rarely wrong. "Where is she?"

"Dev is with her," Alexis answered. "Someone embedded an Ingeniarian tracking device on her, but I was able to disable it. She's resting right now. I know you want to see her, but I think it's more important for you to tell us exactly what happened today at the pavilion. Why are the Ingeniarians after her and what do they want?"

"Some bionic spaceholes chased us into the VR adventure tunnel. We fought. They lost. End of story." He again tried to step past them and was denied. "That's all there is to tell. If we had to stop and explain every time one of us got into a little on-world brawl, we'd never get off this ship."

Lochlann placed a hand on Rick's chest and firmly pushed him back into the commons toward the chairs.

"Blast it, Loch," Rick swore in frustration. "What did you expect me to do? She needed help.

We're helping her. I didn't see you getting all up in arms when Alexis followed me onto this ship while the evil scientists were after her. Or when Raisa was attacked on Torgan and Jackson brought her on board. Or when Josselyn was trapped in a stone prison for a hundred years by the Federation Military. Or Violette kidnapped Dev. Or—"

"Sacred cats, Rick, that's different and you know it," Lochlann countered. "This is the woman who kidnapped you and almost killed you. How did you end up with her again? Did she see you and come after you? Try to finish what she'd started in the Lin Yao Mines?"

Rick gave a dismissive wave of his hand. "I saw her and I followed her. I was curious."

"What is wrong with you? Don't you remember what happened the last time you followed her? You almost died. We were all sure you'd been killed by *chandoo* dealers before we found you in those purple jade mines. We didn't know if we were rescuing you or going to avenge you. We had to fly all over the high skies tracking your kidnapped ass down. Why would you go after her again? You see that *fea*, you run the other way. If you listen to any of my orders, let that one be it."

Rick wished he had an answer for that. The truth was, he hadn't stopped to think. He saw her. He followed her. It was that simple.

"She didn't kill me," Rick said. "She hit me over the head and took me prisoner to keep the other guys from killing me."

"Do you know how insane that sounds?" Alexis asked.

Lochlann took a deep breath as if trying to calm himself. "Are you finally willing to talk about what happened? You get a little weird every time that incident is mentioned, and you were upset when Lucien and Viktor let her escape. We all thought you wanted to torture her for revenge. I for one was relieved she was off this ship for good. I don't like her being back on board."

Rick frowned. "Nothing happened. It was fine. It was fate. I told you before you can't fight fate. If not for that, we would never have gone to Lintian, which set off a chain of events that brought you two together. It brought Violette to Dev, and Raisa to Jackson. And maybe it brought Harper to me.

"Rick, do you expect us to believe that this is fate between you and Harper? Is she how you break your curse?" Alexis asked.

Love? Forever? Those words triggered something deep inside him, a fear and loss that he did not want to look at. "I'm not trying to break a curse. I'm trying to do right by someone who needs our help."

"What *did* happen when she kidnapped you?" Alexis asked.

"Nothing. I said it was fine. It just was a thing that happened," he dismissed.

"Fine?" Lochlann looked as if he was near his breaking point. "You were taken by a drug queenpin and tied up in a dark mine on a remote planet, and you call that fine?"

"I don't remember it all, okay?" Rick shouted, frustrated that the captain was right. "I feel nothing when I think about it. I was in a prison hold, they fed me, I was slapped around a little, and… nothing. It's like this emotional fog. Why do you think I wanted us to take her after you found me in the mines? I want to remember what happened."

"Do you think they did something to you to make you forget?" Lochlann tilted his head, studying Rick as if he could see what was beneath the man's skull.

"This isn't about you, is it? You're worried about her, aren't you?" Alexis touched Lochlann's arm so that she could step closer to observe the pilot. Her eyes slowly changed from blue to purple.

"No, I…" Rick shook his head in denial.

"I've only seen that expression in your eyes a few times. When you thought Lochlann had hurt me. When Raisa was in danger, and we were hiding from the Federation. When we thought we lost Violette on the Zibi fueling dock after we took her back to visit Rifflen to take care of that paperwork. When that random woman on Werten appeared with a blackened eye and a beef-head of a partner." Alexis' smile was tight, and he could see she was trying to be sympathetic. "I worry in this case you're blinded by the fact she's a female. Not all women need to be saved simply because they are women. This woman does not need our help. Her being here poses a threat."

"What if I care about her?" Rick wasn't sure why he said it.

"She said she was betrothed to a prince," Lochlann countered.

"Bucky? No." Rick shook his head, not believing it. "She wouldn't marry a bionic comet-sucker like that."

"And you know this because you became close to her when she was dealing drugs?" Lochlann asked.

"If she was engaged, I think it's safe to say she called the wedding off when she pulled his bio-tubes and disabled his arms," Rick asserted. "She saved me from a potentially lethal blow. Now I want to help her."

"Rick, I'm almost positive that woman is HIA," Alexis insisted. "When I touched the side stitch power source, I could access the Pleasure Droid

Corporation mainframe again. All of it. That thing reactivated the link and I—"

"Are you positive they're not coming after you?" Lochlann interrupted in concern.

"I promise, I'm sure. With the power source gone, I'm disconnected. I wasn't there long enough for them to track me." Alexis lifted her hand and rubbed it. Her pinky was purple and swollen, and Rick wondered at it, but the nanoids inside her would heal it soon enough. Continuing on where she left off before the interruption, she said, "I went down data paths that were so deeply hidden, I'd never known they existed before now. All it took was a commander buying a droid unit for companionship and—"

"So what if she is?" Rick dismissed. "We don't have any trouble with the HIA."

Lochlann arched a brow at the absurdity of that comment. He didn't need to say more.

Everyone who came across the HIA had a problem. The organization didn't like when you knew who they were. Most of the stories about them were probably myths made up to scare people… or not. Rumors surfaced that their clandestine operations took out planetary governments or high-profile aliens who didn't fit a certain agenda. The problem was, no one knew whose agenda was being served. Most aliens didn't want to know.

"All I meant was you said it yourself she had a tracker thing on her. She was running from an Ingeniarian hit squad. I didn't bring her onto the ship. She came to us." Rick kept his gaze steadily on the captain and his wife. That wasn't to say he wouldn't have brought her on the ship if he'd had the chance.

"She's here now and—oh," Alexis stiffened as her eyes widened, "*oh, space balls!*"

Alexis took off running down the corridor. The men didn't hesitate as they followed. Her feet slid as she tried to take a corner too quickly.

"Alexis, what is it?" Lochlann called after her.

"I didn't see it. There was so much information," she said. They approached Dev standing outside one of the prison hold doors. "Dev, open it."

Dev instantly obeyed the plea.

Rick pushed Lochlann as he followed Alexis into the room.

Harper lay on the bed, her face pale and her limp hand reaching toward the door as if she'd tried to get help. Blood dripped from the cot, pooling on the floor and staining Harper's clothing. Her blue-tinged lips were parted, and her eyes peeked through the narrowed slits of her lids.

"What happened?" Rick demanded. "What did you do to her?"

Alexis tried to peel back Harper's bloody shirt. "When it's removed, the side stitch releases a compound that thins humanoid blood. With the wound left from the anchors holding it in, the person bleeds out unless—"

Rick didn't wait to check her wounds as he nudged Alexis aside and lifted Harper into his arms. He carried her out of the prisoner hold and ran toward the medical booth. It wasn't the newest model, and it had been modified more than once, but it should be able to heal her as long as he made it before…

He couldn't think it. She had to live.

The medical booth took up most of the small room. The bed was tilted at an angle so a patient could rest in a half-reclining, half-standing position while the booth worked.

Rick placed Harper inside the unit, knocking her head in his haste. Green lasers lit her body in a scan before he managed to arrange her limbs. His hands shook as he pulled the lid down to trap her inside. He glanced to the control console to find Lochlann had started the unit.

Rick stepped back, staring at her pale features. The gap between where Harper rested and the booth lid allowed him to watch. He breathed heavily, more out of fear than the exertion. His back hit the metal wall, and he slid to the floor.

Harper's chest didn't move. She hadn't moaned when he held her. Her eyes remained closed. Fear unfurled inside him, whispering that he was too late, that she was dead.

"Grab the decontaminator and some clothes," Lochlann ordered. Rick didn't see who he talked to but heard the familiar gait of Dev's footsteps answering the command.

The medical booth buzzed a loud, ugly sound of warning. The lasers shut off, stopping their work. The noise pried his eyes from Harper's face. He'd never heard it do that before, and he surged to his feet to look at the console's dashboard.

"*Deceased*," the console read.

"Shut your black hole, you stupid piece of space junk!" Rick slammed his fist hard on the unit. The screen blipped, and he pressed a button for the emergency protocol.

The lasers turned back on for a few seconds before the buzzer again sounded.

"*Deceased.*"

"No." Rick slammed his fist harder, this time kicking it. He pressed a button for wound care.

The buzzer sounded a third time.

"*Deceased.*"

"Rick," Lochlann tried to reason, his voice calm.

"No." Pain filled him, tinged with anger and panic. "Not again, Sprout. Not again."

Alexis came into the room. She shoved Rick off the console. He hit the wall, only to push himself back toward the controls. He stopped when he saw Alexis rapidly pushing buttons, mumbling to herself, "Relevant to the situation. Alpha. Zero. Reset. Heart. Override. Override. Fry. Shock."

A bright flash illuminated within the unit. A horrible sound came from within, half injured animal, half high-pitched scream.

Alexis poked her finger at the panel and again mumbled, "Shock."

Rick stared at the booth, afraid to move. Another bright flash came at the command. This time the cry coming from Harper sounded more human.

He glanced at the panel. The console screen blinked with alien symbols.

Suddenly the lasers came on, and the unit started to work.

Dazed, and almost too afraid to look, he stumbled past Alexis toward the booth. Harper still appeared pale but her chest was lifting in breath.

"What did you do?" Lochlann asked.

"I'm not exactly sure," she answered, the words shaky. "I heard the death buzzer, and my brain just gave me an answer to try."

Rick reached into the booth to touch Harper's cheek.

"Don't. Let the machine do its work," Alexis ordered. "She's alive but fragile." Then softer, as if talking to Lochlann and not him, she added, "That setting wasn't for a human."

Rick withdrew his hand. He watched the lasers concentrate their energy on Harper's wounded side. The fact she wore clothing didn't matter. A couple of the lasers moved to her shoulder where the killer clown had knifed her.

His heart pounded and felt like the organ had lodged in his throat. He turned to thank Alexis for whatever she had done, but her forehead was pressed against Lochlann's chest, and her shoulders were trembling.

Rick opened his mouth to ask if she was all right, but Lochlann met his gaze over Alexis' head. The captain's look stopped him.

Dev appeared in the doorway holding a change of Rick's clothes and the handheld decontaminator. He paused to look at the woman in the booth.

Rick noticed his bloodstained shirt from where he'd carried Harper. He ran a hand over his arm. The blood had dried, plastering the small hairs down and making the skin feel tight.

"I'm fine," Rick dismissed Dev.

"Don't let her wake up to see you looking like that." Dev placed the clothes on the floor and left. "You don't want to scare her."

The man had a point.

Rick grabbed the decontaminator to clean himself up.

A small, choked laugh sounded, and he glanced up at Alexis. Her eyes were moist as she stared at the clothes. "Yeah, that outfit won't scare her. She'll think she's on a circus ship."

Rick finally noticed exactly what Dev had picked out for him to wear. The orange-tinted tunic shirt and mismatched deep purple pants had been in his drawer next to each other but were not anything he'd worn for a very long time, and never together.

Lochlann snorted as if trying to hold back his amusement. It might have been the nervous energy or the relief that Harper was mending, Rick wasn't sure, but he too began to laugh at Dev's fashion choice. He slid against the wall to take a seat on the floor. When he again looked at Harper, her eyes were opened, staring at him. The laughter died in his throat. Her eyes closed once more.

Rick dropped the decontaminator and stood back up to go to her. He watched her face, willing her eyes to open again and feeling guilty that when she had looked at him, he'd been laughing while she was in so much pain.

7

"Who or what is Sprout?" Alexis asked.

Harper couldn't open her eyes or speak, but she was warm and that was enough for now. Her body rested at an angle, not standing, but not lying flat either. Her weak limbs felt as if they were locked in place. Nerve endings tingled along her side, but at least it no longer hurt.

"When I ran in here, you said, 'not again, Sprout,'" Alexis stated.

Harper listened to her surroundings, trying to figure out what was happening. She recognized the voices and remembered coming onto the ship.

"She's just a girl I knew once," Rick answered.

Harper's body rocked as if the gravity field wasn't as strong as it should have been when a ship flew in deep space. It did not inspire confidence in the old spacecraft.

"Another girlfriend?" Alexis sounded amused. "I guess I should have known."

"It's not like that. I knew her when I was a boy. I was reminded of her recently, but I don't remember much about her," Rick said.

"I don't think I've ever heard you talk about your childhood." Alexis's programming appeared to be very thorough. Harper didn't have many run-ins with pleasure droids, but she could see why people could trick themselves into believing they were real women and not just a bunch of wires and cogs.

Movement sounded and Rick's voice appeared closer than before. "I never met Sprout's parents, but I seem to recall they were scientists at a humanoid facility. Or, at least that's what she told me. She used to sneak out into the forest near our encampment to play. I remember she had a bunch of wild stories and talked about crazy adventures."

Harper felt the warmth moving from her side over the rest of her body. A beep sounded.

"What is it?" Rick seemed panicked.

"I don't know," Alexis answered. "It looks normal, but this panel is all alien symbols, and please don't make me try to translate them."

"Are you all right?" Rick asked. "Earlier, you appeared upset. What was that about?"

"It's nothing. I saw some things I didn't want to see. Sometimes the bad leaks in and I'd rather just forget it."

Harper used the droid's voice to track where she was in the room. She stood apart from Rick.

"What kind of crazy adventures?" Alexis asked.

"Sprout always wanted us to go off into space to do things. Swim Lophibian slime pits. Rescue people imprisoned in stone. Save a prince. Help a princess. Stop planets from exploding. Stuff like that. Oh, and to seek pleasure where I could because life is hard enough."

"She wanted you to be with women?" Alexis asked.

"There are more pleasures to be had besides sex," Rick answered. Then with a small laugh, he added, "Or so I've been told. I think I gave that one my own interpretation."

"You did one of those things when you saved Violette's sister from that Earth settlement turned prison on Florencia's Fifth Moon," Alexis said. "Could be Sprout is out there swimming in slime."

"No." Rick's tone was flat. "She's dead."

"Oh, I'm sorry. How?"

"Shot in the neck. She bled out in my arms. But it was so long ago," he dismissed. "None of that matters now."

"Maybe that's why you're a pirate," Alexis

offered. "You're honoring her memory by having adventures. That could be why you're so protective of women, too. That couldn't have been an easy experience."

"I'm a pirate because I was born to transients and then orphaned," Rick answered. "Like I said, doesn't matter, anyway. The past is done. No need to live there. No need to talk about it."

Harper couldn't resist opening her eyes to look. Rick stood close, but his attention was turned to the side toward Alexis. The orange tint of his shirt struck her as a jovial shade, yet he appeared sad.

She gave a light cough. It jarred her side but was nothing compared to the pain she'd felt with the side stitch. The warmth instantly returned to the location.

Rick turned his attention to her, his face shifting from sadness to one of ease. That mask he wore covered a lot of emotions.

"Hey there, starbeam, welcome back," he said, smiling. "Thought we lost you there for a second."

"I said I didn't want to be in a medical booth," she answered, her voice gravelly. "Get me out of here."

"Beats death," Alexis stated, joining Rick to look at her. "Because there's where you were heading."

"What do you know about it, robot?" Harper

muttered. "Someone unplug your power source once?"

"Robot? No, Alexis is—" Rick began.

"The Alexis Companion model nine-point-seven," Alexis interrupted. "I prefer pleasure droid."

Rick frowned.

"Whatever," Harper mumbled, coughing again. "Get me out of this thing."

"It's not done," Rick said by way of denying her command.

"I'll be fine," Harper insisted, trying to lift her arms to push the top part of the booth away so she could wiggle her way out of the side.

"Stay in there, or I'll make the booth inject you into unconsciousness," Alexis warned.

"I don't take orders from machines," Harper argued. "Rick—"

"Do it. Inject her," Rick told Alexis.

Alexis went toward the console.

"Wait, no!" Harper called out, as she stopped pushing on the booth lid to escape. "Don't do that."

"I get that alien tech can be frightening, but I swear the booth is safe. In our line of work it's been put to the test many times. It's saved all of our lives more than once."

"I'm hardly scared," Harper scoffed. "I just don't want the Medical Mafia having access to my records. I like my privacy."

"Is that because you're HIA?" Alexis asked, her creepy eyes shifting colors.

"What? No, that's ridiculous," Harper lied, keeping her expression unchanged.

Blast it all! How in all the black holes did they figure that out?

"You don't have to worry about this unit transmitting anything. We rigged it so what happens on this ship, stays on this ship," Rick assured her.

"That true?" Harper leaned to the side to get a better look at the robot.

Alexis nodded. "Yes. It's true. We like our privacy as well."

Harper lay back down and relaxed. It made sense that pirates would've found the modifications to block medical booth transmissions. "Okay, then. Why didn't you just say that in the first place?"

"You're going to be in there a while," Rick said. "You want to talk about what happened?"

"No." Harper gave a small shake of her head. "I'm good."

"I'm afraid we're going to need more than that," Rick stated. "What happened after you left me?"

Harper thought about arguing, but finally sighed loudly and feigned boredom. "You told Bucky I wasn't a virgin. I disarmed him to save your ass. He sent his toy soldiers after us. You knocked yourself out on a branch. I hid you under a bed to save your ass. I led the last thug from the adventure hall. I saw you being chased by pavilion security and saved your ass. I got tagged like a fricking animal with a side stitch while saving your ass, and I figured you owed me, so I hopped a ride. You're welcome."

Rick touched his forehead. A light bruise had formed but nothing that would indicate he'd been knocked unconscious by a blow. It wasn't like she was about to admit to injecting him though.

"So…" Alexis came closer, arching a brow. "You two did sleep together when you were pretending to be a queenpin."

"No," Rick and Harper answered in unison.

"Then how did Rick know you weren't a virgin?"

"Lucky guess," Rick muttered.

"Wishful thinking," Harper countered. There was something about this man that made her frustrated and turned on at the same time. Of course, she'd never tell him that she was attracted to him or else he'd never shut up about it until she injected him and made him forget. Again.

"Yeah, you been wishin' to hop on and get a little Rick lovin'?" Rick grinned and lifted his brows.

"You are so…" Harper wrinkled her nose and shook her head.

"Charming? Sexy?" Rick offered. "Attractive?"

"Unfortunate," she answered. "Misguided. Odd."

"Misguided? Trust me." His voice dipped. "If there is anything that I know how to do it's guide my ship in for a landing."

"And with that gem, I'm out of here. I'll check back later." Alexis abruptly left.

"If I hadn't seen her ad plastered all over every fuel dock holograph board, I would have sworn she was alive," Harper stated.

"She is alive," Rick answered.

"I know that you indicated the captain was pretending he was married to the robot, but she doesn't, you know…" Harper glanced down Rick's body. Actually, it was only as far as his chest because she couldn't see farther down than that, but he got her meaning. "*Pleasure* the whole crew?"

"No. She really is the captain's wife, and his kind doesn't share," Rick said.

"His kind?"

"Draig." Rick leaned closer. "He can shift into a dragon."

"That's right. You told me that before, though at the time you had another captain who you said was a catshifter. He was in love with that Lintianese princess."

"Jarek. He and Mei are married now and living in Jarek's childhood palace. Lochlann is our captain now. Naturally, they all begged me to take charge, but I didn't want the responsibility. I like being the pilot." Rick's gaze traveled to her mouth and lingered. "How are you feeling?"

"Like I just bled out all over the floor of your prison hold."

"Yeah, you made quite the mess." Rick sighed as his expression became thoughtful. "We're going to need you to clean that up."

Harper laughed, knowing he wasn't serious. "You're a space cadet."

"I thought you said I was charming."

"I believe misguided was the word I used."

He grinned. "And so we're back to my navigational skills, are we? Can't seem to keep your mind off my great prowess, can you?"

The way he asked the questions dripped with sexuality. A small shiver worked over her, and she closed her eyes.

"What is it? Are you in pain?" His hand touched her cheek. "Is it your side?"

She glanced down. The lasers were concentrating on her ankle. "Let me out of here. My foot's fine."

"Let the machine do its work. It will be finished soon enough."

"Let me out now, and we can have sex," she offered.

Rick stiffened and started to turn toward the control panel only to stop himself. "No. We can't do that. I know I'm irresistible but you almost," he glanced over her and seemed to struggle with his decision, "died."

"But I didn't. Come on. Let me out." Her grin widened. Being near the brink and surviving filled her with a restless energy. "We'll have fun."

He took a step back and lifted his hand. "You, um, just…"

Harper laughed. She closed her eyes and rested her head against the booth. "All talk. No action."

"No, I'm action," he assured her. "But I have a feeling you're messing with my mind again."

Harper opened one eye to look at him. Her heartbeat had quickened, and she felt like her blood was full of fire burning to get out. "A woman can only take so many refusals before she stops asking."

"I'm a little fuzzy on some of the details about the first time we met, but I'm pretty sure I'd remember you offering that as a perk to my prison cell," he said. "I would not have said no."

Harper gave a small laugh, knowing he wouldn't understand the reason for her humor. Rick had no idea about the times they had met in the past, and she had to remind herself of that fact. He remembered the drug queenpin, and as she was now.

Without any injectors at her disposal, she

wouldn't be able to wipe the minds of the entire crew. She'd have to dupe them the old-fashioned way or call her bosses to do a sweep. For the same reason she'd never bring Rick in to have his memories of her erased, she'd not want to bring notice to his crew. Headquarters wouldn't care about a ship of space pirates. It would be easier to blow up the vessel and call it an accident if anyone cared to ask. Spaceships had fatal mishaps all the time, especially pieced-together junkers like this one.

It was all about the greater good.

"Did you fall asleep?" he whispered.

Harper realized she'd closed her eyes and had automatically regulated her breathing as she thought of what she needed to do next.

"No," she answered just as softly. "So if we're not going to do what I want to do, you need to entertain me. When she pulled the tracker off me, Alexis said some weird things."

"She does that," Rick said.

"Why exactly does a pleasure droid know so much about cutting temperatures for Ingeniarian metals used in their bionics?" Harper knew he was going to avoid giving a serious answer before he even said a word.

"She likes to learn things, and we like to take her to trivia contests on fueling dock bars," Rick answered. "Won a laser wrench once."

"I can see how knowledge of the Ingeniare Alliance consisting of three factory planets could be picked up in random conversations or reading a geography book, but I'm not sure I consider in-depth knowledge on the removal of side stitch trackers as common trivia." Harper pressed her knee forward, trying to lift the lid to the booth without being as obvious as before. It didn't budge. "What connection do you and your crew have to the Ingeniarian government? Why were you at the conference?"

Rick laughed. "You think I was there with your Prince Bucky?"

"He's not my prince," she denied.

"Glad to hear it. Lochlann said you claimed to be his fiancée." Rick placed his hands on his hips and appeared frustrated, even as he smiled.

"Well, not me, Harper, but Eloise is," she corrected. "Well, *was*. I doubt the egomaniac is still interested now that you told him I wasn't pure. I have a theory about men like that. It always seems curious when they want a woman who doesn't know what good sex is. Says much about their lack of performance."

"I should be asking you what *your* connection is to the Ingeniarian government." Rick's smile fell by small degrees. "You were pretending to date the prince."

"You first. How did Alexis know about the illegal humanoid transports, or the inherent problems of the working population on two of the planets, or the fact that many of the workers did not sign up for their jobs willingly?"

"You should ask her," Rick said.

"I'm asking you." If she couldn't convince him to release her so they could have some fun, an argument would be the next best distraction. People often revealed too much when a conversation became heated.

"We travel around. I'm sure she picks up conversations." He crossed his arms over his chest and lowered his jaw as he studied her.

"Secret protocols? That's just something a pleasure droid picked up from conversations? Shouldn't she be focusing on tips to please her man?"

"I don't know what you're talking about. I wasn't there when she said whatever it is you think she said. I was busy flying us out of Nozando airspace."

She'd never seen his expression look like the one he wore now. All traces of a smile had disappeared, hidden by a distrustful mask.

"She's talking about the classified file number 7890-8889, which initiates Ingeniarian top-secret protocol for alpha four." Alexis appeared in the doorway. "I had a chance to sort through the information. The directive calls for an infiltration team to undermine the power of the royal Ingeniarian family."

"To save the workers?" Rick asked.

"To cull back their power," Alexis answered. "I didn't find any mention of the workers. Their enslavement didn't appear to be an issue for the HIA one way or another."

They both looked at her. Harper didn't speak. What could she say?

"Have you told the others?" Rick asked the droid.

"Not yet," Alexis answered. "Violette and Dev are finishing up the scans to make sure we're not being followed."

"So that's why you were with Bucky?" Rick stated more than asked. "It's true. You're HIA. Alpha four? So there are three others with you on this mission?"

"You don't want me to answer that." Harper pushed harder at the lid. She needed to find an injector and make Rick forget this conversation.

"His parents controlled three small planets that produced various technological products," Alexis said. "Those products had made them rich, powerful, and bionic."

Harper was tired of the know-it-all droid. The first chance she got she was shutting that thing down. "Just forget you heard anything. You'll erase the droid if you know what's good for you."

"I'm not doing anything to Alexis," Rick denied. He gave a small, humorless laugh and shook his head. "But you being HIA does make sense, doesn't it? Pretending to be a queenpin, pretending to be a pure maiden."

The medical booth beeped and the lid lifted on its own to let her out. Her limbs were a little shaky, but the unit had healed her. Blood stained her clothes. Seeing a decontaminator on top of purple material on the floor, she reached for it. Rick stepped in front of her to block her from picking it up. His leg came close to her cheek, and she felt the heat of him radiate onto her skin.

Harper could think of about three moves that would take him to the ground in seconds—sweep his knee, twist his arm, or grab his face and start kissing. She glanced at Alexis before slowly standing.

"So where do we go from here?" she asked, holding her hands to the side to show she wasn't going to misbehave.

"Alexis, could you give us a moment?" Rick asked.

"I'm not sure I should," Alexis replied. "I don't trust her."

"It's not like I have anywhere to go while we're in the sky," Harper said.

Alexis studied Rick for a long moment before nodding. She left them alone.

"I can't give you the answers you're looking for." Harper lowered her hands and shook her head. "That's not how my line of business works."

"No. I suppose it's not." Rick went to the door and ran his palm along the hand scanner on the wall and tapped a button. The door slid shut, locking them inside.

"You need to stop her from telling the others. The less your crew and your robot know—"

"Alexis was a test subject experimented on by the corporation that manufactures pleasure droids. They used her as a base model to create the robots, as you call them. She's very much alive." Rick took a slow step forward.

Harper eyed him warily. Why was he telling her this?

"You did something to my memories, didn't you?" He came closer.

She kept her place, not moving. When he paused to wait for her answer, she nodded once.

He touched his forehead were the small bruise had formed. "You're responsible for this."

Again he paused, and again she gave a single nod.

"Do you need help?"

Harper kept her eyes focused on his as she shook her head in denial.

"I don't believe you."

"It doesn't matter what you believe." She took a deep breath and strode toward the door. "You can bring me back to my cell now. This conversation is over."

8

Rick went after Harper, blocking her from leaving. He seemed to always be going after her. He saw her, he followed her. It was that simple, and that complicated. She had a pull on him, one he didn't know how to end.

Was it the mystery?

Was it the unfulfilled lust?

Was it something more?

Fate?

Harper frustrated him and confused him. He wanted to shake her and yell at her and make her reveal all her secrets. She was in his head, and he knew there was much he didn't remember about what had happened between them.

His lips tingled as if they knew what she would feel like, even though he didn't recall kissing her.

"You have to let me go, Rick." There was a vulnerability in her eyes now. "If you don't let me go—"

Rick grabbed her by the face and pulled her mouth to his. He had to know if the tingling sensation was right. He kissed her deeply, and she responded as if she knew how he was going to move against her. If she took the memory of their kiss from him, what else had she stolen?

When she didn't resist his touch, he let go of her face and ran his hands along the side of her body, over her hips and around to cup her ass. She held on to him, drawing him closer. Feeling the dried blood on her shirt, he automatically went beneath the material to explore her healed side. His hands trembled at the idea that he'd almost lost her.

"Are you sure we haven't done this before?" His body felt as if he knew her. It was hard to explain. The rest of his body knew something his brain didn't. Every muscle, every nerve, every bone, and blood-filled vein felt her on a metaphysical level. He wanted to absorb her into himself and never let go.

It was his mind that didn't understand. There were so many holes in his memory needing to be refilled.

He kissed her, and it was impossible to feel anger. Desire rampaged through him. Nothing mattered beyond this moment. He dipped his hands into her tight pants, cupping her ass so that she rocked against his arousal. He could have easily met his climax right there, but he held back.

"Yes. We've kissed before," she admitted.

Harper's breasts pressed into him as she tilted her head back to gasp for air. A light moan left her lips.

"I can't seem to stay away from you," she whispered.

"Then stop trying." Rick turned her so she was pressed against the door. He kissed her again, deep and long, showing all the passion he felt for her. Their bodies became a frenzy of exploring movements. She kissed his jaw and neck. He massaged a breast through her shirt. Her nipple puckered against his palm. Her leg lifted to rub against his outer thigh, and the heat of her sex teased him through their clothing.

He needed to be inside her.

Harper tugged at his shirt. He broke the kiss and let her yank it over his head. He then removed her blood-stained shirt and tossed it aside.

Rick kneeled before her and slid her pants down her body, revealing the long, athletic lengths of her legs. The hair guarding her sex caused a groan to escape him. He nipped at the front of her thigh while trying to lift her feet from her boots. She ran her hands through his hair, forcing his kisses to move upward.

Harper's right leg pulled free, and he lifted her by the back of the knee. Her leg hooked over his shoulder. Rick trailed kisses along her inner thigh toward her sex. The second his lips encircled her clit her hands clutched his shoulders for support. He delighted in her taste. His arousal strained against the binding material of his pants begging to be liberated.

Rick was confident of his skills as a lover, and he poured everything he had into giving her pleasure. When he felt her start to tremble against his mouth, her hand urging him to stand, he dropped her leg and surged to his feet. His fingers fumbled to release his cock.

Every movement was mindless. Her fevered breathing and soft moans begged him to hurry. He lifted her by her thighs, pressing her to the door for balance.

When he entered her, it was unlike anything he'd ever felt. Intense pleasure flooded him with each thrust. He felt her muscles clenching and unclenching against his shaft. He wanted it to last forever, but the moment she tensed, crying out with release, he joined her. His climax hit hard. They stayed pressed together, panting for air.

"I know this was a mistake, but I don't care." Harper inhaled a deep breath and pushed hair away from his face to look into his eyes.

"How can you call this a mistake?" he countered. "It feels right to me, and I think it feels right to you too. Admit it. There is something between us."

He might not remember having sex, but his body remembered her. This is where he wanted to be. There was no logic, no reason he could voice. It just was.

She smiled, but the look didn't reach all the way to her concerned eyes. "I'll admit that it was fun and I definitely want to do it again, but it's only going to make it harder when I have to leave."

"Oh, don't worry, we'll definitely do it again, soon and often." Rick grinned as he pushed away from the door. His pants were around his ankles, and he pulled them up before handing his shirt to her to replace the bloody one.

"I have a job to do. If I get back to it, hopefully my bosses won't know I veered off track."

He'd do anything to erase the sadness from her features. "We'll help you with that."

"I can't allow that," she denied.

"You can't stop us. When the rest of the crew hears that people are enslaved and being forced to work, they'll want to stop it."

That was what they did. They helped people.

"You can't speak for the crew in this matter," she denied. "It's too dangerous."

"I doubt they'll say no. How about you tell me all about the mission on the way to my quarters?"

"You were never supposed to get involved, Rick," she whispered as if afraid that someone, somewhere, would hear the confession. She hugged the shirt to her chest.

"Too late. I'm already involved. I'm helping whether you ask me to or not, so you might as well ask for it."

"You were supposed to believe I was a criminal." She shook the shirt out and began threading her arms into it. "You need to believe it. You need to forget about me. If I can complete my mission, I might be able to hide what happened on Nozando. I can protect you. All of you. But to do that, I have to finish what I started."

When she had his shirt covering her body, he unlocked the door and peeked out into the corridor. He took her hand and pulled, leading her toward his room. Once inside, he shut the door and began removing his boots. He needed to feel her again. He might never get enough of her.

As if the conversation hadn't stopped, he said, "So what's the directive? To overthrow a government?"

Rick had no interest in taking down governments unless it meant helping those who were currently being harmed by that same government. If they didn't help the workers, then a new dictator would just move in and take the old one's place.

"Lessen their power," Harper corrected. "I know what Alexis said she read, but I was planning on doing whatever I could for the workers. It might not have been written in the directive, but I am well aware of their plight. It's why I was trying to get close to the prince. It's a delicate situation. We don't need the Ingeniarian technology, we just need to temper back the power of those who produce it."

Rick gave a small nod. "Sounds simple enough. After we…" He gave a seductive glance over her body and winked. "I'll let the others know we have a new adventure. Maybe we can scavenge some tech while we're at it. Any of the Ingeniare planets should have plenty of it lying around. We are pirates after all."

Harper arched a brow. "I'm sorry. When I said *we*, I meant my team and me. You and your friends aren't coming anywhere near this operation."

"Like we'd let you have all the fun." He swept her into his arms and tossed her onto his bed. Being as he had been solo on the ship, the bed wasn't huge, but it served its purpose. A laugh escaped her at the sudden, playful act. "Now let me tell you about my plan. First, we need to get you out of that shirt. It's only going to get in the way of my current mission."

9

A pirate crew meeting was definitely a far cry from an official HIA briefing. They gathered in the commons, the brothers Lucien and Viktor making a wide arc around the room to keep away from her. Evidently, by their expressions, they had not forgiven her from escaping on their watch. They did not meet her gaze.

The captain sat with his men, appearing no more in charge than Dev or Jackson or any of their wives. Rick insisted Alexis was alive, and it was believable, but after all those transmissions, it was difficult to see anything but an expensive toy. Raisa appeared the friendliest of the bunch, smiling and looking like she was on the verge of a thousand questions.

"So what kind of food did your family eat?" Raisa asked.

Yep. Questions.

"Uh, crops," Harper muttered, vague on purpose.

"But the dishes you made with the crops?" the woman persisted. "Were there any traditional items? Maybe something you made on holidays?"

Harper glanced around the crew. They watched her expectantly. Was this some kind of test? What did her childhood diet matter?

"Mostly nutrient paste from tubes, I guess," she said at length.

Raisa's expression fell a little. "Oh. That doesn't help."

"Are you…hungry?" Harper asked. "Do you need me to show you how to work a food simulator?"

Raisa made a small noise of surprise before she began to laugh, prompting everyone to join her. Harper frowned. They acted like she'd just told the funniest joke they'd ever heard.

Rick's hand slid onto her lower back, his fingers caressing her. The gesture was more possessive than she was used to. He leaned close to her when he explained, "Raisa is an Intergalactic Culinary Specialist. She practically invented all the recipes in a food simulator."

"That is hardly true," Raisa protested. "Only like an eighth of them. And I won't be working for Simulator Corp much longer if I don't get something in to them soon. They'll try to take my molecular gastro-spectrometer away."

"They can try," Jackson threatened his wife's non-present bosses, "but no one threatens my love's molecular gastro-spectrometer."

Was grumpy spaceman being… playful?

"Here. Here. Sorry." A woman entered carrying an electronic clipboard. Her hair was pulled back to rest in a mess of brown curls at the nape of her neck. "I thought I saw something on the scanner but it ended up being what looks like part of an old ship floating in the black. I tagged it in the computer, but I doubt it's worth the time it would take to haul it in anywhere."

The woman handed the clipboard to the captain who instantly passed it to Viktor, who began poking at the screen.

"You must be the untrustworthy queenpin who stowed away on our ship and brought the threat of the Ingeniarians on us that I've heard so much about." Green eyes met Harper's. "I'm Violette Craven Stephans en Dehauberkelsain en Thoraxian en Yyrtolzx Devekin."

It was clear which man Violette had paired herself to with that Bevlon surname.

"You must be the woman who isn't qualified to be flying Rick's ship," Harper quipped.

"Call me Violette." The woman winked.

"Harper," Harper answered. She instantly liked the woman. Though playful in tone, she carried herself like she'd been through some kind of agency fight training.

"Wait, Rick's ship?" Lucien laughed. "Sam might have something to say about that."

"Who's Sam?" Harper looked around the group, pretty sure she'd picked up on everyone's names.

"Princess Samantha was our captain before she decided to stay on Qurilixen. This is her ship," Dev stated, before instantly changing the subject. "Am I correct in believing that the Ingeniarian threat has been stopped by the disarming of the tracker?"

"So far," Violette said. "I had to divert some of the resources from other parts of the ship to give us enough power to scan on all frequencies for the time being."

"What did you turn off?" Viktor asked, concerned.

"VR." Violette leaned over to kiss her husband's cheek. "Sorry, Dev. You'll have to find another way to train."

"But I was in the process of loading a new program," Viktor said.

"Then that explains why it was drawing so much power," Violette answered. "You'll just have to do it again later."

"Did you pick up new programs at the conference?" Jackson asked.

Viktor smiled. "Maybe."

"What kind?" Raisa asked. "More combat scenarios?"

"Sure," Viktor said.

"If we could talk about the current threat," Dev inserted.

"Good idea," Lochlann seconded. "Alexis discovered something about our new friend."

All eyes turned to Harper. While watching the banter between the crew, she'd enjoyed having the attention off her. Now it was back, reminding her she was an outsider. Normally that fact didn't bother her. For some reason, here, standing beside Rick and his crew, it did.

"Do you want to tell them?" Alexis asked.

Harper didn't speak.

"All right." Alexis stood from where she leaned against her husband's chair. "Harper is an HIA agent, and she needs our help to free a planet."

Any remains of a jovial mood faded.

"I didn't ask for help," Harper said.

"A whole planet?" Lucien clarified, as they ignored her statement.

"It's home to a factory of roughly five hundred workers," Alexis said. "And maybe around thirty or forty guards."

Rick dropped his hand from her back. "The workers at the Ingeniare Three factory are being forced to labor against their will. Some are criminals, but many are those who dared to defy the Ingeniarian government."

"So not a whole planet, just a factory?" Lucien asked.

"The factory is pretty much all there is on the planet," Harper stated.

"All right." Lucien sat back in his chair and nodded.

"It's part of the Ingeniare Trio," Alexis explained. "The original planet, Ingeniare One, where the population lives, shouldn't cause a problem. Ingeniare Two is where the factory headquarters are located and where they keep their laboratories. We might have an issue with them because they closely monitor the Ingeniare Three and regular transports between planets."

"If we can get that transport schedule, we can try to time our plan accordingly," Dev said.

"And I'll need anything you can get about the security systems," Jackson added.

"I'll work on that," Alexis acknowledged.

"We might be able to jam communications

between the second and third planets," Lucien said with a glance at Viktor.

Viktor nodded. "We could rig something to mimic space noise like we did when we were trying to pass through," he glanced at Harper, "places undetected."

"We can put out a signal with my father's Federation code if it comes to it," Violette said. "If they check it, we'll be screwed, but that might buy us some time if we're found."

"What about the HIA?" Jackson asked. "Will they offer support?"

"HIA doesn't care about the factory workers. They want to derail the Ingeniarians' power," Alexis said with a sidelong glance in her direction. "They're infiltrating the royal family and the laboratories."

"That isn't true," Harper defended, feeling as if she was under attack. "If it were as easy as walking into a room and flipping a switch, I would have taken care of it by now. You're talking about a very powerful ruling family whose scientists literally invented half of the biotechnology currently used, hundreds of monitored workers, security systems, bionic guards, the list is endless. If we can strike a blow to the family's power, we can stem the flow of their production. No production, they won't need to gather more workers. From there we can focus on the other problem. I don't know where a pleasure droid model got her information about this secret mission, but just because it's not in the mission file doesn't mean it isn't a concern. And you need to be careful. If they find out you're tapping into a private database, they will come after you."

"I'm not—" Alexis began. Lochlann touched her arm to stop her. She patted his hand. "It's fine. The fate of five hundred workers is more important than any secrets I may have."

"My wife isn't a droid," Lochlann said, giving Alexis a small smile as if making the statement proved his support of her decision.

"Pleasure Droid Corporation used me as a base model for the Alexis droid. It's easier to imprint the programs off of a live subject," she said.

"I already told her," Rick admitted.

"I meant base model. I've never heard of a woman volunteering to be used in such a way," Harper said.

"It wasn't a volunteer position." Alexis took a deep breath. "What happened, happened. It's not important. What *is* important are the results. They filled me with uploads, and I was attached to the Pleasure Droid Corporation's mainframe by remote access."

"That's disconcerting, but I don't know how that explains how you know of the HIA files." Harper studied each of them in turn. Maybe her first impression of them had been hasty. She'd taken them for petty criminals.

Alexis rubbed her temple.

"Millions of files," Lochlann said. "Alexis is a living computer database. She knows practically everything—navigation, ship schematics, biomedicine, scientific studies, cultures, and customs. More than any human brain was supposed to carry."

Harper's eyes widened. She could imagine the type of experimentation that would be done to make such a thing possible.

"Pleasure droids collect information about their owners, and when they're recharging, they submit reports. Pleasure Droid Corp is not just about making people happy and sex robots. For centuries people have known that the most valuable thing in the universes isn't technology. It's information. The powerful need it. The greedy sell it and use it. And they get it all for the low price of a little physical pleasure." Alexis' eyes continued to change color. Really it was the ultimate disguise. No one would think about a pleasure droid walking around. They were laughed off as jokes.

"So someone who knows about my mission has a droid?" Harper asked, almost angry that some commanders need for sexual release resulted in her mission being compromised.

"We severed my attachment to the mainframe, but when I touched the side stitch power source, the surge it caused reactivated that connection. I was thinking of the Ingeniarian tech and that thought process brought me to a tiny wormhole into the HIA database, and to your mission. When I stopped touching it, the connection severed but not before I'd downloaded more information. I've been sorting through it."

Alexis risked much admitting what she'd done. One hint to Harper's bosses that the pirates had accessed confidential files and the entire crew would be blown out of space.

Harper noticed something strange as they spoke. Not one of them questioned if they should help. They all automatically assumed that they would.

Relying on her judgment and gut instinct, Harper decided to trust them. There was no point in lying about her mission since it sounded like they could find out everything on their own, anyway.

She studied Alexis. "Did you see all of it? What it's like on Ingeniare Three?"

By the woman's expression, Harper instantly knew she had read the information packets attached to the files.

"What?" Dev prompted.

"The working conditions are tightly packed, dark, and the hours long. We saw the trackers first-hand. They bus them to work, they bus them home to sleep," Alexis said. "The exposure to the machines leaves them vulnerable to diseases. If they become sick too often where trips to the medical booth are slowing down production, they're disposed of and replaced like a bad part."

"Tell them the rest," Harper said to Alexis.

Alexis' eye color flashed faster than before, as if she was accessing the information. She flinched as if someone had punched her in the stomach, though no one had moved. Lochlann rubbed his wife's arm in a comforting gesture.

"Roughly every five years they do a full worker purge," Alexis said. "They think it keeps any information the workers may have learned as to how to defeat their captors from being passed along. It's called uprising management."

"That doesn't sound pleasant," Violette said.

"The file came with images. It's not pleasant." Alexis closed her eyes briefly, and when she opened them the color change had slowed. "That's why we need a plan now—even if it's a long shot. By my calculations, they're due to purge the current workforce."

"Then we have no choice," Rick said. "I'll set a course for Ingeniare Three."

"If we're going to do this, there is a big problem we need to consider," Harper said. "All the factory workers have the side stitch. Mine was in for a short time. Some of them have had theirs for years, and they're fused to the bone. Even if we had time to remove them all, one by one, they'd bleed out. We don't have enough medical booths to handle the population."

"We'll need a way to disarm them all at the same time," Lochlann said.

"I'll work on that," Viktor volunteered. "I have the broken side stitch. I'll reverse engineer it to figure out how it works so we can disarm them faster."

"There has to be something we can give them before we take them off to stop the bleeding," Rick said.

"Maybe through the local food supply," Raisa offered. "I'll go through my notes and contact Jobby to see what food sources are on file for that region." She glanced at Harper. "Jobby Dawks is my food simulator contact for turning in recipes. He'll have listings for the region we'll be in. It's a long shot, but I'll try."

"While you're waiting for the answer, do you want to help me with the tracker?" Viktor asked her.

Raisa nodded.

"I'll try to see what information I can find about how the side stitch power source works to help you," Alexis added. "Maybe if we can shut that down without removing it, we won't need to take them out."

"You need to be sure so it doesn't set off an explosion," Harper warned.

"What about a device called the eight crystals? I saw a reference to them being able to polarize… something," Alexis suggested. "Is that an alternative power source we can—?"

"No," Harper denied. "The crystals are not what you think they are. Trust me, they won't help. It's impossible to even gain access to them."

"Everyone knows what they need to do. Rick, chart our course and check the scans," Lochlann ordered.

"What about me?" Harper asked. "I can help with the scans."

"No," Lochlann denied. "I need you to stay with Violette and Alexis. Tell them whatever you can about what we're walking into."

Harper hesitated a moment at the way he gave her an order before slowly nodding.

The mood was much more solemn than when the meeting had started. As the men filtered out of the commons, Rick remained beside her.

He touched her cheek. "Thank you for trusting us."

"I don't have much of a choice," Harper said. "But I have to know why? Why would you all risk yourselves for this?"

"Because it's the right thing to do." Rick gave a small shrug. "We are but specks in the universe for a short time. We might as well make that time count for something. Saving a planet full of people seems like as good a way as any to meet that end."

Violette and Alexis took a seat away from them, waiting for Harper.

Harper studied Rick's face and just knew this moment would be one of very few in which they would be together. He was right, the universe didn't care about them. Their paths were never meant to cross, and yet they did. They were random elements bouncing into each other. The odds of surviving this were small, and if by some miracle they pulled it off, they would have to go their separate ways. HIA didn't have much of a retirement plan.

"Find me when you're done here." He leaned to kiss the corner of her mouth.

Harper stiffened at the touch, trying to steel her emotions. He gave her a strange smile and she watched him leave.

"So, you and Rick?" Violette prompted. "Is it serious?"

"I take this whole situation seriously," Harper answered, not feeling comfortable discussing her feelings. It was hard enough keeping what she felt for Rick in check. Every time he was near, her heart leaped a little, and she wanted to go to him. And, each time she saw him, she needed to stop him from following her. Her life's path did not include real relationships, not when she had to contend with so many fake ones.

"I know that Rick comes off charming and flirtatious. We've seen women fall for him, but he hasn't attached himself to any of them. I think it's his confidence." Violette said, her tone matter of fact.

"Did you and Rick...?" Harper frowned, wondering at the advice. Was that jealousy?

"What she means is Rick can come off like he has the attention span of a glartnat," Alexis said. "He's all fun and flirty—"

"Unless he knows a woman is taken," Violette interrupted.

"Yeah, if she's taken, he'll treat them like she's his little sister, or mother, or some other nonsexual entity." Alexis motioned that Harper should sit with them. "I don't think we're explaining ourselves well. The point is, we care about him. We don't want to see him preoccupied with what-ifs and romances that won't ever be if you're not serious about him.

There is too much at stake. We won't lose our families to distractions. But if you truly care for him…"

Alexis let her words taper off. Both women looked expectantly at her. What did they expect her to do? Become all girly and start gossiping about how she felt? Confess that being with Rick, even *near* Rick, caused her to rethink everything she'd ever believed in? The crazy fool kept saying he loved her, and by all the universes, she wanted to say it back but the words would hurt too much.

"I understand." Harper took a seat. She gave a half-version of the truth. "Love is the last thing I'm looking for. I long ago accepted the path I've chosen means I can't have certain things. The only thing I can think about right now is how to get everyone through this crazy mission alive."

Violette relaxed her posture, but she didn't appear happy. "Now that's settled and we know where you stand, what do we need to know about what's ahead of us?"

Rick felt a tickle beneath his nostril and swiped at his nose, coming away with a smear of blood on his thumb. He stood at the end of a cliff, looking out over a clearing beyond the forest. His knees locked, though it would hardly protect him from a strong wind. He peered down, seeing his toes hanging over the edge and the great distance awaiting his fall.

"Are you better now?" Sprout asked. "I'm sorry if your head hurts. I should not have tried that last upload."

Rick's head throbbed violently. With the uploads Sprout had stolen for him from the facility where she lived, his brain was packed full of new knowledge. "It's better. A headache is a small price to pay for the knowledge to fly us off this world someday."

And in the moment, as the upload unpacked itself into his mind, he knew which ship would take them away the fastest and how to fly it into the high skies.

"I know you will fly away. I won't be with you." Sprout rarely talked about her life, and he didn't pry, but he innately understood she felt as stuck in her circumstances as he did. "Do you think we'll be friends in the life after this?"

Sprout's voice sounded small.

"I don't think there is anything after this life," he answered. Her small hand fit into his. He knew this memory wasn't right. He was a grown man, and she was a foggy recollection from childhood. His hand should have been smaller to match hers, as he'd been a boy when this had happened. "We will make the most of this one."

"If I disappear, don't follow me," she whispered. "I hope you're wrong about the next life. I want to see you again."

"If you disappear, I will find you," he promised. "There are so many adventures to be had. You're coming with me. I don't care what your parents say. We're leaving this place together."

"Promise me you won't forget everything we talked about, Rick. Get into trouble and don't let anyone stop you." Sprout's thin shoulders shook before she lifted her chin in resolve. She tossed the uploader over the side of the cliff and watched the expensive piece of equipment crash. "When I'm gone, you have to do all the adventures. Don't forget."

"Stop talking like that," he dismissed.

"Promise me, you won't follow," Sprout insisted.

"No." He shook his head. "What is this about?"

"I have to go." Sprout took off and sprinted into the trees.

Rick automatically gave chase. She moved quickly for a girl as if each little leap of her legs propelled her twice as far as it should. He jumped down the incline that led away from the cliff's edge. He ducked under trees, knowing there was a place he needed to be. If only he could find it.

"Rick." Sprout's voice was strong, commanding his attention.

He turned toward the sound. Sprout's dark eyes met his as she stood on a small path that cut through the litter of the forest floor.

"Promise."

He nodded once. He tried to speak, but the shot from a blaster cut off his words. He knew what was coming, and he tried not to see it. When he turned his back, it was only to find her still standing before him. There was no escaping. Sprout's eyes widened, and she grabbed her neck. Blood filled the nooks between her closed fingers, pooling before spilling over in a stream.

"How can you sleep at a time like this?"

Sprout's lips didn't move. She started to fall.

"Rick."

He gasped and jerked upright in his pilot's chair in the cockpit.

"Seriously, that must have been some dream," Violette said.

"It was," Rick began to explain, still foggy-brained and trying to capture the details before they faded back into dreamland. "I was—"

"Nope. No. Not a chance," Violette cut him off. "You were making strange little moaning noises. I don't want to hear about how some Galaxy Playmate was stroking your ego."

"It wasn't a Galaxy—"

"Seriously, no. Don't care. Don't want that image in my head." Violette went to the console and began checking the course he'd charted.

He shook off the sickening feeling he'd woken up with and forced a playfulness to his tone that he did not feel. "Don't trust me?"

"No, I trust you, mostly," Violette answered. When she'd finished checking his route, she hummed thoughtfully.

"What?" He pushed up from the chair to look at what she'd found.

"Nothing. It's perfect," Violette said.

"Just like me," he answered, winking.

"Ugh, save it for your current fling. I think she's waiting for you in your quarters." Violette shooed him away. "Go sleep in a bed. I'll take the night shift."

"Don't mess with the controls," he ordered. "I have them how I like it. And don't reroute any power without checking with me first. You nearly fried the spare board."

"What spare board?" Violette asked.

"The one I put on to keep you from diverting power from my room." Rick laughed as she leaned over to look beneath the console. "You'll never find it."

"You might want to stop Harper before she starts snooping in your drawers," Violette returned. "I shudder to think about what she might find."

Rick held up a finger to retort, but then muttered, "Yeah, you're probably right."

He made a show of hurrying from the cockpit just to make Violette laugh at him. When he entered the corridor, he kept jogging, wanting to see Harper.

As Violette said, she was standing in his room waiting for him, the door opened. He slid into the frame, grinning. "Greetings, love. How was your meeting with the ladies? Did you talk about me?"

Harper's lip twitched up at the corner. "Yes. We did."

"Did you tell them how good of a lover I am?" he asked. "I'd understand if you'd want to brag about that but be sensitive to the other guys. We don't want them to feel bad about themselves."

Her smile widened. Damn this woman was beautiful. He felt drawn to her, an invisible wire that plugged him into her. The upcoming insanity hung over the ship, but that was nothing new. They'd faced dangerous missions before—albeit not one as crazy as taking on an entire planet of biotech to save hundreds. That part was new.

"Your sexual prowess didn't come up," she confessed, "but they told me you were charming with the ladies and not to get attached to you."

"Well, too late for that, obviously you're attached." He lifted his arms to the side, letting her look her fill. "Once you've had Rick, you don't want anything else. It is the burden of my life that I must carry."

"Your modesty is astounding," she teased.

"You have no idea." He stepped inside, waving his hand over the sensor to shut the door. He pulled at his shirt, tossing it aside before putting his hands on his waist. "You want to see what else I have that is astounding?"

"Your collection of junk." She went to a shelf where he had placed several items he'd collected throughout his travels. Lifting a metal star, she asked, "What is this stuff?"

"Twenty-first century Old Earth memorabilia," he answered. "That is called a badge. Old lawmen used to wear it. At least, in the transmissions they did. The transmissions are called movies. Some are even whole stories. People collect and trade them. We often catch old wave fragments while flying around. If you can get a good one no one has seen before, that's where the money is."

"Huh, you don't say," Harper drawled, not looking too impressed. She set the badge down. "Why twenty-first century Earth? What's so special about it?"

"Because it's freaking awesome," he exclaimed. "Aren't you curious about the place where most humans started?"

She ran her finger over the edge of the star, not picking it back up. "I'm more interested in where we're going and how we're getting there."

"I think you have to understand the mistakes of the past in order to make a better future." He took her hand in his and tried to lead her toward a viewing screen. "If you're nice to me, I'll let you watch one."

Harper crossed over to him. "So if I'm mean to you, you won't make me watch them? Promise?"

"You're funny," Rick said. "I promise the action ones are beyond the stars good."

"I guess everyone needs a hobby." She still wasn't convinced.

"Let me show you one of the transmissions before you judge. I think you'll be surprised at how awesome they are. Soon you'll be begging me to find you more of them to watch."

"Doubtful." Harper grinned and touched the inside of his thigh. "Besides, I already have a new hobby."

"Yeah." His voice lifted an octave as she glided her hand upward. He cleared his throat. "That's a pretty good hobby, all right."

"I thought you might like that."

Rick studied her for a few seconds before leaning over to sweep her up into his arms. He carried her toward his bed and set her down gently. He climbed over her to lie along her side, their bodies close.

Rick stroked her cheek, letting his thumb glance along her mouth. "Why did we wait so long to come together?"

"Who says we're together?" Harper whispered.

The words might have been meant to keep distance between their emotions, but the way her eyes gazed at him said she wanted more, much more. He leaned forward, brushing his lips along hers in a deep, slow kiss. The passion between them burned. Her hands strayed over his naked chest, up his arm and along his neck. Each glide of her flesh to his made his body erupt in awareness.

His breathing deepened. He pulled away to peel the clothing from her body. He wanted to touch more, to press close and feel her warm skin and eager heartbeat. He wanted to hold her against his chest and keep her there.

Rick had been with women, lots of women, more than he could count. The universes were vast, and he had explored them greatly and with enthusiasm. None of that mattered. All the others paled to this moment, mere blips on a radar screen that would fade into nothingness. Never, in all his lifetime, could he remember such a strong pull toward another person. Never had he been so sure of what he felt.

When he finished gently undressing her, he pushed roughly out of his pants and threw them from the bed. Her eyes met his, and that adorable half-smile beckoned him to resume kissing her. She felt the wire between them. She had to. They were two circuit boards in the same system.

Why was he thinking in electronic metaphors? He must be tired. He'd have to work on that before he told her how he felt.

He kissed her briefly, unable to deny her needs.

"I love you," he whispered. The confession rolled out and he was unable to contain it. So much for thinking before he spoke. All the same, he didn't want to take it back.

Her hand instantly left his shoulder and pulled back as she moved to touch her inner thigh.

He leaned away to follow the gesture. "Is something wrong?" The view of her parted legs wasn't bad, so he remained where he was.

"Um…" She seemed a little out of sorts as her fingers worked against the smooth flesh of her leg as if searching for something. He'd evidently said I love you too quickly.

"Allow me." Rick pushed up from the bed and pulled at the blanket to force her to roll onto her back.

Harper gave a surprised laugh.

He moved between her legs. Using his tongue, he licked and kissed her inner thigh before moving to do the same to the opposite leg. "Mm, beautiful."

"You make it impossible to think," she whispered. Her feet dug into the bed as she tried to entice his lips upward.

Rick took his time exploring her, not wanting

the moment to end. He kissed down her legs before returning to the apex of her thighs.

Harper gripped his hair, tugging his face against her sex. She arched against his mouth, crying out in pleasure as he tasted her. Her foot pushed along his arousal, rubbing near his hip.

The universes faded until all that was left was this bed and this woman. He moved up along her body, needing to be inside her again. Her nails raked along his back to his ass, finding hold as he came above her. Their lips met in forceful passion as if each tried to consume the other. Hands moved everywhere they could reach, gripping and stroking. Tiny moans sounded from their throats.

Rick tried to savor the moments, but they became faster and faster until each touch, scratch, bite, kiss blended into mindless perfection. He kept his hips back, kept from entering her, as he made sure she built toward her climax.

Harper rolled him onto his back and straddled his waist. This was a woman who took want she wanted from him, and he was happy to let her. Rick would do anything for her—protect her, help her, give his life. That was the only way he knew how to love.

There was a desperation to her movements when she drew his cock into her depths. He'd had many fantasies in this room, but they all paled to the reality that was Harper. Her head tilted back in pleasure. He held her hips and watched her breasts as she moved.

Rick wanted to give her every part of himself. Her hands dug into his chest. The second he felt her tremble in climax he joined her with his own hard release. He held her hips tight against him.

The tremors subsided, and her hands slid from his chest to press into the mattress. She gave him a brief kiss, her breath falling heavy against his cheek.

"I told you I was astounding," Rick whispered as she rolled off him.

"And still so modest," she answered with a laugh.

He wished she would say she loved him but would happily settle for any admission of affection. Instead, she closed her eyes.

"We should sleep while we can," Harper said. "Who knows when we'll get another chance."

He moved onto his side to give her more room on the smaller bed and put his arm around her waist to keep her next to him.

"Did you figure out when we'd arrive?" She snuggled into him.

"We have about two days, depending on our final route," he said. "It's a good thing, too. Any longer and we'd have to detour to a fueling dock."

"You do know attacking the Ingeniare Trio is

insane, don't you?" She opened one eye to look at him.

He gave a small laugh to hide the worry he felt. Now that he knew what she was up against, there was no way he'd let her go on alone. "Insanity is part of the fun, starbeam. If it wasn't dangerous, everyone would be doing it."

11

"Are you sure this is something your crew wants to do?" Harper stared at the viewing screen. The deep blackness of space was a familiar sight, and still if she allowed herself, she could see the immense beauty in the expanse of stars. A smear of magenta and purple dust cut across the darker sky. The nebula appeared brighter than most she'd seen. "You don't have to. I can tell you where to drop me off, and I can continue on alone."

She knew Rick's answer before he said it, but she had to offer.

"I already told you, babycakes, we're not letting you have all the fun." He winked at her before returning to the long list of numbers he was analyzing on an electronic clipboard. "Besides, you may need me to save your ass again."

"I think I was the one doing most of the saving," she answered.

"That's because you like me." Rick didn't look up.

I love you. His words echoed in her head.

"It is beautiful, isn't it," Harper said with a small sigh, watching to see if he'd give her his attention. Every time he looked at her, he smiled. "Up here in space, you can almost believe that the universes are a wonderful place."

"Mm-hmm." He didn't glance up at the nebula.

"What are you looking at?" She moved to lean over his chair.

"I sent a small probe out to see what's in that thing," Rick said. "My gut says to fly around it, but that will burn more fuel and take more time."

"You think it's manmade?" she asked, looking at the bright lights. Usually, a nebula's gravitational pull didn't bother a ship, and they could fly past them without noticing anything beyond a beautiful view.

"I think," he pointed toward the viewing screen, "that center is suspicious. It looks like someone is trying to set up a new planetary system out here, and they've accelerated the process." He gestured at a block of the numbers on this clipboard. "See, none of this is reading right. If we fly too close, it could knock out our power and pull us in. I am handsome, and I know the ladies like to look, but I don't want a new star cluster named after me quite yet. The Rick galaxy will just have to wait."

"You're just…" She gave a small laugh, knowing he was joking around.

"Yeah, I know." He grinned even as he kept looking at the readings.

She moved back to stare at the bright center. "I've heard of aliens trying to do this. I've never seen it though."

"I don't see a name for it in the star charts," Rick answered. "I'm going to tag it as the Harper Nebula when we go past. Named after the prettiest lady I know. And I'll have a picture of your lovely face pop up each time a passing ship reads the geotag."

It was almost too sweet.

"I'd rather you pick a nickname instead and not include the picture," she said. "All it will take is one cartographer ship charting the sky, and I'm screwed. I'm not sure I can do my job if everyone starts recognizing my name and face."

"Nickname for Harper, huh?" This time he did glance at her. "Harpy Nebula it is."

She began to smile, only to stop as she saw his smirk.

Leaning over to the controls, she hit the comm button and asked, "Does anyone know what a Harpy is?"

Rick pressed his lips tightly together.

"Old Earth monster," Alexis answered. "Human lady head, claws, wings, greedy, thought to epitomize an unpleasant woman."

Rick began to laugh.

"Thanks," Harper said, cutting the comms. Chuckling, she kicked at his leg. "You're a space cadet."

"Yeah, but you still like me," he said.

I love you.

She wanted to hear him say it again, even though she knew it was wrong to encourage the sentiment. They could have moments where they forgot the danger they faced, but it was always there, looming in the background. Harper wished there was a way she could escape the ship and go on without them. She did not want their deaths on her head.

I love you.

Every time he said those words to her, no matter the meeting, he sounded convinced. She wondered if he fell in love with every woman he was attracted to or just her. The only difference with this time was, she had been unable to jab him in the leg to take the memory of his realization away. Now those words hung awkwardly in her mind, paralyzing her emotions.

Love.

In her line of work, love was a dangerous thing, even the love of family and friends. When she spoke of her childhood, it was never "her" childhood. It was a made-up story, an alias, a tool to endear her faster to her mark. It was a means to an end.

"My parents were poor," she said, not knowing why. "They gave me up to a finishing school because they thought that would give me a better life."

Rick set the clipboard on his lap and looked up at her, not answering.

"It did, and it didn't. They didn't let the students contact our families until we finished the program. For years, all I could think about was the day I would graduate and return home. Depending on my age, I'd had so many speeches planned. I'd yell at them for not giving me a choice. I'd thank them for their sacrifice. I'd tell them it was all a waste and I wanted to come back home forever. I'd tell them…"

I'd say I love you. I understand why.

"What?" Rick prompted.

"So many things," Harper answered.

"Which did you end up saying?"

"None of them. When I returned, I found out my parents had been dead for six years. No one told me. My mother had given birth to a boy about six months after they sent me away. He died too. The royals had put everyone on rations. There hadn't been enough food. Half the village was wiped out. I had no one. So, when the HIA asked, I said yes on the condition my first assignment would be the downfall of that royal family. Now *they're* poor and on rations."

"I'm sorry you lost them." He stood and reached for her, pulling her against him. His arms wrapped around her shoulders as he held her close.

Harper didn't cry. Those tears had dried up long ago, but the hollow ache inside her chest remained. It had been clear her mother had been pregnant, and that would have played into her parents' decision to turn her over to the school.

"If we're going to die doing this, I wanted at least one person to know my story," she said.

He nodded as if understanding the need.

"My parents are both gone now, too," Rick shared. "They were good people. We were transient, traveling around with a caravan. They didn't aspire to much, they didn't ask for much, and they didn't have much. I was raised outside, staring up at the stars as they told stories around a campfire. My mother died from what I can only assume was a lifetime of drinking and eating whatever she wanted. She was a tough woman. My father was lost without her, and he kind of just withered and faded. He was stabbed during a card game gone wrong. First chance I got after that, I hopped on a transport and never looked back."

"Is that when you met up with Sprout?" Harper pulled back to study his face. "You are a restless sleeper, and you've said the name."

"I met Sprout shortly after my mother died. She was probably my best childhood friend even though we didn't know each other a full year. I found her in the forest one night after she'd snuck out of her facility home. We were instant kindred spirits. Her parents were scientists."

"What kind of scientists?" she asked.

"I couldn't tell you. I'm not even sure if her name was Sprout. I just called her that because when I found her, she was pulling tiny sprouts out of the ground and holding them up to the moonlight like they held all the universe's secrets inside of them. She must have traveled everywhere, though, because she knew about many things. In some ways, it felt as if she'd predicted parts of my future. She talked about people in stone, and we found prisoners on Florencia's Fifth Moon who had been stuck in a stone-like state for over one hundred years, abandoned on a dead settlement by the Federation. We saved the only survivor, Violette's sister."

Harper watched his face, detecting hints of the emotions he tried to hide.

"A few times when we met, she'd brought an uploader with her that she took from her mother's laboratory," he continued. "That's when I first learned to fly. At the time, I didn't always know what I was learning, but she'd give me all the information she could find, loading it into my brain until my head throbbed and my nose bled. She called it a temporary discomfort to a lifetime of advantage."

"What happened to her?" Harper had heard his conversation with Alexis when the medical booth was working on her injuries and knew the child was dead.

"I never found out for sure why, but someone shot her in the neck with a blaster. I tried to help her, but she bled out. She'd been worried about something the last time we talked. My father came and swooped me under his arm and ran me away from there. He refused to speak of it and would tell me to push it from my mind, to never mention it, to never think about it, to never go looking. So, that's what I did. I boxed it up, shoved it deep, and managed to forget for a time. But when you left me with the demon spawn in the VR tunnel, I started to remember. Now it's stuck in my head and keeps leaking into my dreams. I'm sure whatever my nightmares are trying to tell me will work themselves out one way or another."

"Do you think she stole an upload she shouldn't have?" Harper asked. "Something with sensitive information?"

"Not that she ever gave to me." Rick caressed Harper's cheek. "I have accepted that sometimes life does not give you the answers you seek, and it's best not to look for them or else you'll go mad. I can't do anything about the past, but I can do something now."

The hollow feeling from her past didn't leave her but the pain it caused eased as he held her.

"You keep asking if we're sure like none of us have thought this through." Rick released her and went to pick up his clipboard. "Everyone on this ship has a story. We all have our losses and our reasons. We chose this life. We need this life. Without this life, we are nothing. Pleasure Droid Corporation, Federation Military, the ESC, the HIA, Ticaran nobles, blood drinkers from Kintok secret laboratories…it comes, we take it on. If we stop helping, if we stop fighting, then we might as well stop breathing."

Harper nodded in understanding. "I won't ask again."

Rick returned his attention to the clipboard. "Would you check the radar? We'll be heading into interference soon, and I want to make sure we're still clear of your ex."

"Ugh, don't call him that." Harper gave a small shiver of disgust. She pulled up the radar and leaned close to the display as she flipped through the different channels. "I can't tell you how many times I had to knock him out and take away the memory of it when he started annoying me."

Rick began to laugh, but the sound stopped suddenly. "Wait."

She glanced to find him touching his head where he'd hit the branch. It wasn't the most artful of segues, but she felt like she needed him to know the full truth if they didn't survive this.

Realization dawned in his eyes as he looked at her. "You knocked me out."

Self-preservation told her to lie. In no way would this confession make her look good. Instead, she gave him a wide, frozen smile. "Radar appears to be clear. I should check again, though."

"Harper," he demanded.

"Are you sure you want to hear this?"

"*Harper.*"

"Things are going so well between us."

"You took away my memories, didn't you? You knocked me out."

"Not with a branch. You did that to yourself," she confessed. "I just…"

"Just?"

"Nicked you." She waved her hand in dismissal as she turned her back on him to continue checking the radar.

"You *what* me?"

She felt him moving behind her and straightened. She didn't turn to look at him. "I injected Swipe into your thigh and made you forget your time with me, or part of the memory, anyway. It's standard HIA issue. I tried to erase the adventure tunnel, but you moved and I spilled half of my last dose."

Rick pulled at her shoulder to turn her around to face him. He studied her expression.

"Trust me, it's better than my bosses coming in to do a full mind-wipe." She wished she could walk the conversation backward.

"That's why I don't remember much about the first time we met."

"Do you mean the mines?" Harper asked.

Rick nodded.

"Yeah, sorry, that wasn't the first time we met. It was, um," she tried to do a mental tally, "the fourth? Fifth time, maybe? Let's see, there was the fueling dock when I was pretending to be a waitress, the space station, Torgan poker game, Torgan Scavenger Hunt finals, the jade mines, and now Nozando. Oh, and once at an animal trade show."

"I've never been to an animal trade show," Rick stated.

Harper gave him a guilty smile. "Did I say I was sorry?"

"Wait, so you just love me and leave me? Is that the deal?" Rick arched a brow. "I'm not sure how I feel about that. Though it might explain the deep connection I feel toward you."

"No. We never had sex before this time. We flirted with the idea, and I thought maybe we would a few times, but there were always people around." Harper bit her lip and glanced away. "Every time you see me you try to talk to me. If I didn't stop you, my team would. It seemed kinder to make you forget."

"I can't tell if you're joking or not."

"The first time you almost wrecked my mission, I thought it was a chance encounter. You weren't the first patron to proposition me. Luckily, I was just gathering intel and didn't lose my mark because we were in a diner. The second time I considered a fluke since it was at an animal trade show. I believe your crew was going to see the Galaxy Playmates and you took a wrong turn. The third time, I thought you were messing with me and remembered who I was because the odds of you finding me again on a space station were astronomical. You almost cost me my arm, by the way. You called me babycakes and distracted me while I had my hand jammed inside a time-lock vial drawer. The time you and your crew were competing at the Torgan Scavenger Hunt, you asked if I wanted to see you release your giant caged beast."

"Oh yeah." Rick gave a small laugh.

"You remember?" she asked, surprised.

"Not meeting you, but I remember the line. I'm sure it would have worked if we hadn't been in such a hurry to get out of there. We had Prince Falke, a catshifter, in a cage in his tiger form. The man is terrifying. My captain was pregnant, and it became this whole ordeal. But we did win the hunt." He waved his hand as if stopping himself from telling the rest of the story. "You were saying."

"Next, we met again on Torgan at a poker game. I was losing at Frendle's Chips. You offered to make me a winner." She arched a brow. "Not one of your strongest lines."

"I can't believe that didn't work," Rick protested. "Are you sure you didn't ravish me and are just too embarrassed to admit how I rocked your world?"

"Yeah, I am embarrassed to say that line did work. That time we were on the way back to my room when my partner on the mission found us. I had a lot of explaining to do. Finally, I convinced him that you were in the way of my true target and

I was luring you to my room to incapacitate you. Which I did. Sorry."

He shook his head as he rubbed the back of his neck. "I'm not sure I want to remember all the times I didn't get lucky."

"You should remember the mines… mostly," she said. "You were with me too long to erase everything so I just took what I had to. Anytime you overheard something you shouldn't have, or we started getting a little too amorous. Depending on the dose, the Swipe injection affects short-term memories. Usually, it's just an hour or so before the event. I tried to make you forget the VR tunnel, but you jerked and caught me by surprise and I was unable to finish giving you my last dose. If what I've deduced is correct, you only forgot realizing you love me… again."

"Hmm." He nodded slowly.

"Why aren't you mad?"

"About what?"

"I nicked you. I didn't want to, but I felt I had to. I took away your memories. You can't be happy about that." Harper didn't understand this man. "Anyone else would be raging at me right now for what I did to them."

"I'm not happy about it, but I can't change the past so why rage about it?" He shrugged dismissively and seemed more interested in staring at her mouth. "I know enough about the HIA to understand you probably saved my life, possibly the life of my crew as well."

"I never did it to your crew. I always managed to avoid them when we met," Harper said. "Well, not in the diner, but then they didn't try to follow me into the back room like you did and catch me on a communicator. They didn't remember me when they thought I was a queenpin."

He nodded as if contemplating everything she'd said.

"I am sorry." Harper's hands trembled. This nervousness she felt was an unfamiliar sensation. Standing before Rick, with the truth of who she was and what she had done laid out before him, made her vulnerable. His opinion of her mattered.

"I don't suppose there is a way to get those memories back?" he asked.

"There have been a few rare instances where the memories have resurfaced but mostly in small pieces or like deja vu." She placed her hand on his chest. "I'm sorry."

Rick pattered her hand before letting his rest over it. "I believe you. I've done things I've regretted so I can't judge."

"Like what?"

"I insulted an ancestral spirit and brought a curse down on the crew. Well, not Lucien and

Viktor, but Lochlann, Dev, Jackson, me, and our pal Evan, who lives on Qurilixen with his wife."

She eyed him. "Now I can't tell if you're joking."

"It's true."

"I don't believe in curses." She gave a small laugh. "Someone was probably just trying to scare you with superstitious nonsense."

"I wouldn't say that to the rest of the crew," Rick warned. "They believe they broke their part of it."

"What exactly was the curse?"

"An read our futures and said five of us would find true love represented by five Lintianese elements, but if we weren't careful, we might miss the signs and be forever alone."

"Elements?"

"Water, fire, metal, wood, and earth. I think the real curse came from overthinking, which could have ruined their chances."

"Their chances?" Harper clarified.

"I regret the worry the curse put on my friends, but I tried not to think about it."

"And what element are you?" she asked.

"An didn't tell us who was who. Clearly, I'm metal, because I'm strong as steel and I fly this ship. Or maybe fire, because I'm so hot I burn." He winked at her. "Those two make the most sense."

"And there is no way you'd be earth, water, or wood," Harper teased, finding this whole conversation bordering on ridiculous. Curses were not real. Now, this An person could have had some psychic powers. Those were documented enough in the galaxies. It would be enough to make someone believe a curse was real.

"Not a chance. Raisa was buried alive, so I'm pretty sure she's earth," Rick dismissed.

"But, by this reasoning, you did knock yourself out with a branch. That's wood," Harper answered. "And you drink water. And you were in a VR field so that's earth. And the ship is metal. And—"

"Poke fun at us all you want, but I'm telling you, the prediction curse has come true so far," Rick insisted. "All I know is, I will never anger the spirits on Lintian again."

Harper found herself wondering what their element might be. It was silly, of course, and she pushed the fanciful thoughts out of her head.

"Harper, I am no saint, and I'm not angry about what you did," he kissed her gently before continuing, "but don't nick me again. If the HIA is going to come for me, tell me. Give me the choice to run or stay. Let me remember why."

"I want to promise that but…" She took a deep breath. "Yeah, okay, I promise."

The trembling in her hand subsided under the

warmth of his palm. He closed his eyes, and the corner of his mouth lifted. A soft moan left him.

"What?"

His grin widened and he peeked at her from under one eyelid. "Since I'm missing those memories, I'm just filling in the blanks myself." He gave a small moan of appreciation. "Damn, starbeam, you are quite the wild one, aren't you? Can't get enough of—"

Harper laughed as she jerked her hand away, only to hit him on the chest.

"If you're done in here, set the autopilot." Dev appeared at the door. "Captain wants everyone together to go over a plan."

"We'll be done in a moment," Rick said, turning his attention back to the clipboard.

Harper took her cue and began rechecking through the radar frequencies. A tiny blur caught her attention. "Uh, guys, what's this?"

When she glanced up, Dev had left. Rick came over and looked. He tapped the radar display a few times with his finger. The blur disappeared. "Could be noise from the nebula."

"Could be?"

"Yeah, could be." The tone of his voice was easy, but she saw his eyes narrow slightly as if he didn't want her to be frightened. That was a sweet gesture, but she was trained to deal with fear in its many forms.

Rick swiped his hand over his electronic clip-board before tapping it against the radar. The unit absorbed the information and synced to the display. A small holographic radar hovered over the device.

"We'll keep an eye on this." He selected several buttons and hit a switch on the console before motioning toward the door. "Let's see what every-one's come up with."

She grabbed his arm to stop him from leaving and tried to speak.

Rick shook his head. "Don't ask again if we're sure about this, starbeam. Whatever happens, it's not on your head. We are living the life we chose."

That wasn't what she was going to say. In fact, she wasn't sure what she wanted to say to him, only that the words were stuck in her throat.

I'm sorry.

Don't die.

I'm not good when it comes to love.

I'm not scared of death, but I'm afraid of what I feel for you.

Harper nodded. "Yeah, okay. I won't ask again."

12

"Do you want the bad news or the really bad news first?" Viktor held up the shell of the side stitch for everyone to see. They'd assembled in the commons. Aside from the captain's private quarters, it was the only room big enough to comfortably hold everyone.

Raisa stood beside him, not appearing too pleased. She had been helping Viktor analyze the Ingeniarian tracker. Her brow furrowed in worry. Jackson was near her in a chair. He reached out to caress the back of her arm, and she moved toward him.

"Just give us the news," Rick said. He couldn't help glancing around at his family. That's what this crew was—family.

Lochlann and Alexis were squished together in a

chair that was not made for two. Her hip lifted against his as she settled next to his side, and her leg draped his thigh. Violette sat by herself with Dev standing behind, as if to watch over her. Lucien perched at the end of his chair, wringing his hands.

They had faced many dangers before. They'd crash-landed a ship from space. They'd been shot at, beat on, kidnapped, tortured, and left for dead. And even with all of those collective experiences, there was something different about this time.

Harper.

Harper was what was different.

"Our problem is the shell. The metal is designed to protect what is inside from attack. I found a way we can disable all of the trackers at once without having to remove them," Viktor said.

"How is that bad?" Rick found himself moving closer to where Harper stood. He started to lift his arm around her, but her glance stopped him.

"It requires a sonic blast—and the level of ultra-sound frequencies we need will also kill everyone in its path at the same time." Viktor released the disabled side stitch from his fingers, only to catch it and hold it in his fist.

"That's one way to free them," Lucien muttered, not impressed with his brother's idea.

"I checked in with Jobby," Raisa said. "The factory worker diet on record is basically nutrient paste and a couple local fruits. We only found the records for a few food simulator sales to that third planet, so there's not any way to produce mass quantities to give out. There are a few foods on the main planet that would help counteract blood thinners if consumed over time, but it's not practical. Any other alien foods we'd want to introduce to do the job are too far away. It was a long shot to begin with and it doesn't look like it will pan out."

Alexis lifted her hand and held her palm toward Viktor. After a few seconds, she said, "Let me see that."

Viktor placed his fist behind his back and shook his head in denial. "No, I have the power source inside it. I don't think you should come near it."

She stood from where she sat next to her husband. "I know. I can feel its energy."

Viktor looked at the captain for confirmation as Alexis came toward him. Lochlann nodded once.

Viktor lowered it toward her outstretched hand slowly. "Please don't make us break your fingers again."

Lochlann moved to stand behind his wife as Alexis placed her hand around Viktor's fist. She gasped, and her eyes began to flash wildly through the color spectrum before glazing over.

"Ow, holy space balls," Viktor grumbled as

Alexis squeezed. "I didn't want you to break *my* fingers instead."

Lochlann held Alexis against his chest as she gave a violent shiver. "Viktor?"

"I got it." Viktor grunted, clearly in pain.

Alexis held on to him and began going through her sequence. "Biological warfare using audio waves, base frequencies employed. Irrelevant to the situation. Reexamine. Experimental uses of advanced sonic weaponry in a military environment for disabling humanoid opponents' central nervous systems. Irrelevant to the situation. Reexamine. Bioeffects from high and low frequency sonic exposure as seen on Janex Nine patients. Vestibular damage. Hypothermia. Intense pain. No cure found after tissue damage had been done to the population. Irrelevant to the situation. Reexamine…"

"How is that irrelevant?" Harper asked. "I think killing people with our rescue tactic is very relevant."

"It's just her programming," Rick said. "It's irrelevant because that thread of information doesn't help us find the solution we need."

Harper crept closer to Alexis as the woman kept mumbling through her findings.

"…reverse engineering of bio-targeting devices…" Alexis mumbled.

Harper lifted her hand in front of Alexis' face and gave a small wave.

"She can't see you," Lochlann said, a little annoyed.

"…impractical on a large scale. Irrelevant to the situation. Reexamine…"

Harper pulled her hand away. "I've never seen anything like this."

"Don't get any ideas, HIA," Lochlann warned. "No one is taking my wife from—"

"Harper is not going to tell her superiors about Alexis," Rick stated, coming to her defense.

"I'll kill anyone who tries to take her," Lochlann stated.

When Rick would argue the point further, Harper gave a small wave of her hand to stop him and said, "I don't blame you for not trusting me. I wouldn't trust me either if I was in your position. All I can say is that I wish none of you harm. You allowed me to stay on the ship when you could've thrown me into the black and not thought twice about it. I owe you a life debt for that. Prince Bucky would have enjoyed torturing me if he had caught me. Even more importantly, Alexis saved my life when she removed the side stitch and repro-grammed the medical booth. I do not take that lightly."

Lochlann nodded, but his concern for his wife

kept him from looking one-hundred percent convinced.

"Of course," Lucien interrupted. He and the rest of the crew had been focusing on Alexis while Lochlann had been warning Harper. "Viktor you should have thought of that."

Rick turned his attention back to Alexis to see what she was saying.

"...magnetic pulse. Relevant to the situation. Modified electromagnetic pulse. Relevant to the situation. Old Earth antiquated technology. Irrelevant to the situation," Alexis said.

"Wait, go back," Viktor ordered, his voice strained from the hold she had on his hand.

"We need to get her out of the database. She's staying in too long," Lochlann said, still holding his wife. "Pleasure Droid Corp will track her if they find her poking around in there."

"Alexis, get schematics on building a modified electromagnetic pulse large enough to disable the trackers in one blast," Viktor said.

"With no loss of humanoid life," Violette added.

"Minimum of a fifty-mile radius," Harper put forth. "That's the size of the factory, including security offices and living quarters."

Alexis kept filtering information.

"Alexis, it's time to get out of there," Lochlann

ordered. He reached for her hand locked over Viktor's.

Without his help, Alexis released Viktor's fist. Her eyes cleared from the haze and she took a long, deep breath as if steadying herself.

Viktor dropped the tracker into his free hand before he stretched and shook his crushed fingers. "Damn. I can't feel my hand. Next time someone else is holding the power source."

"Are you disconnected?" Rick asked Alexis.

She gave a slow nod. "The casing around the device helped. It was strong enough to connect but allowed me to disconnect myself." Alexis rubbed her forehead. "I think I might have an answer but I need time to sift through all of it. I grabbed as many files as I could. Some are in alien languages I'll need to translate first."

"Put that somewhere safe," Lochlann told Viktor with a meaningful glance at the power source.

"What's with the clipboard, Rick?" Violette crossed toward him.

Rick lifted the device to show the holographic radar still floating over the surface. "Harper noticed a blur. We're monitoring it to make sure it's a space anomaly and not a ship following us. I should also mention the nebula might be manmade, so we should fly the long way around it. That will put off our arrival time by about a day."

Violette leaned closer. Dev and Jackson were instantly behind her.

"I don't see anything," Dev said.

"There." Jackson pointed.

Rick held the clipboard so that it laid flat. All eyes followed the radar. The soft ping appeared in a streaky blur.

"What is that?" Violette leaned closer still. "I don't recognize the shape. Rick?"

Jackson poked his finger into the hologram as if that would help make the images clearer. It sent a ripple over the image.

"No clue," Rick answered.

"Are we going to be attacked again?" Lucien asked, not moving from his seat. "Tell me now so I can start stockpiling food into the secret laboratory."

"What secret laboratory?" Harper asked.

"Shut up," Viktor grumbled at his brother.

"He's just running his mouth," Jackson dismissed. "Ignore him."

Rick wasn't about to lie to Harper, and he needed his crew to see that she could be trusted.

"Before we became in possession of this ship, a Hungariz man had paid the Kintok captain to hide him and his wife in a secret laboratory hidden behind the corridor walls," Rick answered.

Each time he looked at her, he caught himself staring. She was so damned beautiful, and he wanted little more than to find an excuse to get her alone.

"She had contracted an illness. He grew old trying to find a cure and couldn't take care of her," Raisa added, "so the husband put her into hypersleep before he died until we came along and woke her up."

"Only, what was in there wasn't his wife," Alexis said.

Harper arched a brow, doubtful. "And where is this Hungariz lab?"

"Hidden," Raisa said.

"With a blood lock," Violette added.

"This sounds like a pirate tale meant to scare me," Harper dismissed.

"It's true. We can show you," Violette offered.

"We do not go in there," Dev stated.

"It is not safe," Jackson added. "What was done in that place is not to be reactivated. It is best we let the reserve power run out."

"I agree with Jackson and Dev," Lochlann said. "Leave the laboratory alone. No one is to go inside unless it's an emergency."

Violette smirked. Raisa patted Jackson's arm. Alexis rolled her eyes.

Rick knew the ladies would ultimately do what

they wanted even if they respected their husband's opinions.

"What a strange ship," Harper whispered to him.

Rick grinned, sliding his arm around her.

Violette took the clipboard from him. "I'll watch this." She began tapping the digital buttons. Suddenly, music started playing over the ship's comm system. The rhythm was strange and mellow. A woman began to sing, the alien words sounding both hopeful and sad.

"Oh, there it is." Jackson grabbed Raisa's hand and spun her into his arms. They began swaying as he danced her around the commons.

"My lady?" Lochlann bowed toward his wife. Alexis slipped her arms around his neck and held tight. He straightened, keeping her close as her feet dangled over the floor. Violette kept hold of the clipboard to watch the radar. Dev slipped a hand beneath her knees and lifted her against his chest. He swayed as she rested the clipboard over the bend of her stomach and thighs.

"Harper, may I—" Lucien tried to ask.

"Back off," Rick ordered. He grabbed Harper's hand. "This one's mine."

Lucien shrugged. He closed his eyes and began swaying on his own, lifting his hands into the air as he dipped his head. Viktor went to find a bottle of Old Earth whiskey and poured himself a glass.

Rick placed Harper's hand on his shoulder and pulled her into a dance. He wrapped an arm around her, pressing a hand against the small of her back. He brushed a strand of hair from her face before cupping a cheek. They swayed to the rhythm.

No one spoke over the song. A soft *tink* came as Viktor refilled his glass. He lifted it toward Rick in a salute before taking a long drink.

There were very few moments that struck Rick as perfect, but this would be one of them. They were all together. They were alive. Harper was in his arms. Tomorrow might bring sorrow, but there was this moment.

The song didn't last as long as he wanted it to. When it finished, the spell it created lifted and, as if by unspoken agreement, they began to filter out of the commons. Harper stayed close.

"Let's finalize a plan," Lochlann stated. "Everyone knows—"

"We got to fly," Violette shouted as she practically jumped out of her husband's arms. She dropped the clipboard onto the floor. "Not a blur. Not a blur!"

Rick let go of Harper as he ran after Violette. The hard clank of metal grates reverberated beneath them.

Violette was sliding into the copilot seat when he came into the cockpit. She brought up the radar for him to see as he took the controls out of autopilot, canceling their current route. The blur had formed into an unmistakable shape.

"Who's crashing our party?" Rick asked. He grabbed the flight controls and braced his foot against the floor.

"Medium craft. Not Federation," Violette answered. "Trying to pull up better visuals."

Rick pressed a button for the ship-wide comms and said, "Ladies and gentlemen, this is your handsome pilot speaking. Hold on to your asses. We're going to do a little fancy flying this fine dark afternoon."

He left the comms open, not wanting to stop flying to mess with announcements.

Rick glanced at Violette. She gave him a nod, strapping herself in. He waited a few seconds to let everyone brace themselves before he jerked the controls. The nose of the ship dove downward into deep space. The nebula left the corner of the viewing screen, replaced by the empty black.

Gravity controls destabilized, and he lifted in his seat before they slammed him down once more.

"Whoo," he yelled, jerking the controls again as he turned the craft into a hard left.

He leveled out, and they both watched the radar

to see what the ship would do. The sound of Violette's breath punctured the silence as they waited.

"Maybe they'll pass us," she hoped.

For several seconds it continued on course before sharply turning to follow. A tiny blur lit up the radar, zooming toward them.

"Or fire on us," Violette ground out as she furiously worked the controls. "Pull up!"

Rick took her advice. They felt the partial impact as it struck. The ship groaned as the blast skittered across its belly.

"Those bastards try to hurt my girl? Don't you worry, we'll take care of them." Rick patted the ship's console once before returning fully to the controls.

"Analyzing blast," Violette said, ignoring his strangeness. "Nothing is pulling up in our records."

"Alexis said the energy felt Ingeniarian." Lochlann's voice boomed over the comm a little too loudly.

Fainter, they could hear Alexis' voice mumbling, "...irrelevant to the..."

"Rick," Harper's voice sounded on the comm, "if it's Ingeniarian, fly toward the nebula. Bucky tries to avoid them. He claims the natural interference messes with his bio arms."

"Thank you, starbeam." Rick shifted directions,

aiming for the nebula. "Vi, I need you to divert power. We're making a run."

"We don't know what formed that," Violette warned. "You said you thought it was manmade. How sure were you of that?"

"We have two choices, nebula or blasters." Rick had determined there was about a twenty-five percent chance the nebula was harmless. He chose not to repeat those odds out loud, seeing as how Prince Bucky and his bio-guards were zero percent harmless. "The way I see it, the best case if Bucky overtakes this ship is that we find ourselves stitched up and working in a factory for the rest of our lives."

Violette pulled up a viewing screen. "Diverting power now."

"It's about to get dark," Rick announced to the crew. "Strap down and hold on."

His heartbeat quickened, and he zeroed in on his task. This is what he lived for. He knew his ship, and he knew the skies. Knowing Harper was on board only made him more determined to keep everyone safe. Bucky might side stitch most of the crew and put them to work, but that was nothing compared to the torture he'd dole out for a woman who had betrayed him. Men like that were always the same—spoiled little rich boys who were never denied a thing in their lives.

The lights from outside the corridor flickered and darkened.

"Ready," Violette said.

"Almost, almost…" He pulled the controls, lining up his new flight path. "And… now!"

Violette slapped her palm down on the control that would initiate a power surge and held it firm. The ship jerked before speeding up. The metal walls began to shake.

"Come on, baby, come on," Rick pleaded. "Give it to me, baby. Come on. Just a little faster."

The nebula began to fill the viewing screen as he aimed toward its center.

"We're starting to get interference." Violette released the control before she started slapping her hand on the console.

"Hey, easy on my girl," Rick protested. "She likes a gentle touch. Don't you, baby?"

"I'm not sure if I should be jealous of a ship," Harper's voice piped in over the comms.

Rick grinned. "There's plenty of Rick to go around, ladies."

"What does she see in you?" Violette muttered even as she gave him a quick grin. She punched the console with her fist. "Dammit. Radar is out. We're flying by sight."

The viewing screen flickered, disrupted by whatever was creating the nebula as they neared the space dust.

"We're flying by feel," Rick corrected.

"Rick," Dev's voice warned.

"Don't worry, big fella, I got this," Rick answered. The viewing screen went completely dark. Rick pushed the comm button, shutting it off so the others couldn't hear what was happening. "Let's not tell them we're flying blind."

Violette braced her hands and nodded. She alternated her attention between the dead radar and the viewing screen as if willing it to come back on.

"Rick?" Lochlann's voice sounded.

Rick ignored the captain. He eased the ship to the left, trying to visualize where the nebula was. Suddenly the lights flickered off, and they were in pitch black. He felt the hum of the engine as the ship continued through deep space. Metal rattled so hard his seat vibrated.

"Rick?" Violette whispered.

"Just a little more," he answered, hoping he was right. He eased the controls to take them farther to the left.

"We're too close," she insisted. "We're burning too much fuel. We can't keep this up."

The engine stuttered as if to second her concern. He eased left, feeling the ship's responses to him. He pictured Harper's face in the nebula, tracking where it should be in the darkness.

"Violette?" This time the voice was Dev's.

"Sorry, buddy. Can't find the comm controls," Rick answered, knowing the man couldn't hear him. The engine stuttered again, jerking harder.

"What can I do?" Violette asked.

"Just a little more. Come on, baby." Rick shut his eyes in the darkness. The longer he could keep the ship on course, the better chance they'd lose their tail.

Sweat beaded his brow and rolled down his temple. The engines sputtered.

Please, baby, he silently begged.

The engines cut out completely. Gentle reverberations of metal sounded behind them as they lost speed. Violette's breathing became harsh in the darkness.

"Blasted," Violette whispered. "No, no, no."

"Don't move." Rick unbuckled his strap. He ran his hand over the console, feeling his way around the controls. As if on instinct, he began flipping switches and hitting buttons. If there was one thing he knew, it was this ship and how to fly it.

He also knew that this time, he might have pushed it over the limit.

The vibrations quieted. Without power, they were floating in the black. It was possible the nebula would suck them in and spit them out as part of a new planet.

He counted to ten before hitting the ignition.

Nothing.

"Rick? What can I do?" Violette insisted.

"Don't you worry," he assured her, hoping he sounded confident. He began flipping switches again. "I got this under control."

He thought of his crew, the only family he had. Everything he cared about was on this ship. Maybe he should have tried to outrun Bucky. At least then they wouldn't be floating dead in the sky.

He hit the controls again.

Nothing.

He tried a third time. His hands shook. They couldn't go out like this. Not like this. Not because of his flying.

Please, please, please…

Nothing.

Fourth.

Nothing.

Fifth.

Nothing.

The ship was dead.

Rick took a deep breath, the sound choppy even to his own ears. Sweat stung his eyes, and he blinked hard. He needed to think of something.

"Rick?" Violette begged, her panic mounting.

He couldn't bring himself to lie so he didn't answer.

Sixth.

Nothing.

Come on, baby, don't do this to me.

Seventh.

Nothing.

He tried a new approach, hitting the controls in a different sequence.

Still nothing.

Nothing.

Nothing.

Rick straightened his shoulders as he stood in the darkness. Tears threatened his eyes. His hands shook. He was out of ideas.

"Rick, what can I do?" Violette commanded, her voice stern as if to knock him out of his own head. "Let me help."

Harper. Violette. Alexis. Raisa. Lochlann. Dev. Jackson. Lucien. Viktor.

The faces filled his mind, and he knew he was responsible for what was about to happen. Lack of food, or lack of oxygen, or the artificial nebula's pull —it was anyone's guess which would get them first.

The pain and fear built inside him until it erupted in a frustrated growl. He kicked the ship hard, jamming his toes into the underside of the console. Violette gave a little scream of surprise.

He opened his mouth to apologize for what he'd done, knowing it would not make the reality better.

The lights finally flickered, and the console came on.

Out of everything he'd tried, kicking worked. He stared at the viewing screen in disbelief as the image of the artificial nebula lit up the cockpit.

"There she is. That's my girl." Rick attempted to sound at ease even though he was still shaking.

"What did you do?" The magenta glow cast Violette's face in a soft light.

"I told you not to worry. I'm the best pilot there ever was," he answered, forcing a grin. They both turned their attention to the radar and watched. The unit's display fluttered but the blur following them was gone. They'd done it—at least for the time being. "Let's steer out of here. With any luck, Bucky and his bandits will think we're dead in the sky."

"Looking for a new course." Violette still sounded a little shaken as she pulled up the star charts.

"What's happening?" Lochlann demanded over the comms. "Are we hit?"

Rick pressed the button to answer him. "All good, Captain. Everything going according to my plan. Stay strapped in just a little longer. We might hit some turbulence."

He turned off the comm.

"Some plan," Violette muttered. "I saw the look on your face when the lights came on. You were as surprised as I was."

"My eyes were adjusting to the light."

"Sure. That must have been it." Violette was unconvinced.

Rick began to take his seat to fly them out of danger when he remembered what he'd told Harper. "Oh, wait."

He went to the panel and began typing.

"What now?" she asked.

"No other ships are ever going to get this close." He grinned as he launched a geotag into space, far enough to keep it from being sucked in too soon, but close enough to keep anyone else from bothering to destroy it. "I hereby dub this the Harpy Nebula."

"You're a space cadet," Violette chuckled. "Come on. Let's get out of here."

The food Raisa placed on the table in the ship's small mess hall looked like nothing Harper had ever seen come out of a food simulator. The colors were vivid, and it lacked the usual manufactured smell that tinted most simulated foods. But that didn't mean it appeared appetizing. "Try it and tell me what you think. I think I finally have the molecular structure right."

Viktor sat at the table next to her as Raisa tried to feed the two of them.

If they could call this food.

Harper lifted a brown, narrow piece of what could have been a sort of protein. It sat on the plate next to a pale-yellow mixture. It smelled good, but she wasn't sure she wanted to put the piece of alien food into her mouth. "What is it?"

"Bake on," Viktor answered, taking a piece. "Like it's baked on the bottom of a pan, and the burnt part is scraped up in strips."

Harper wrinkled her nose. That didn't sound delicious at all.

"Bacon," Raisa corrected. "I discovered it on this tiny settlement that drew its roots back to something called Midwest, Old Earth."

Harper broke off a piece and slowly touched the tip of her tongue to it. A strange, salty flavor assaulted her mouth, and she gagged. She instantly dropped it. Shaking her head. "No."

Raisa frowned. "Really? Everyone else seems so taken with it. What do you normally eat?"

"Have any nutrient paste?" Harper wiped her hand against her mouth, willing the taste away.

Raisa wrinkled her nose in disgust. "I hope you're joking. That was perhaps the worst thing to happen to the culinary arts. What kind of foods do you remember from childhood?"

Since answering "tree root soup" seemed a little too depressing, she instead said, "Nutrient paste."

Raisa carefully schooled her expression. "Were your parents... *scientific*?"

"No. They were poor." Harper gave an uncomfortable smile, wishing for anything to interrupt this conversation that she did not want to be having about her childhood. "I was taken in by a boarding facility, and they fed us paste."

What she wouldn't give to have the lights cut out again, trapping them in darkness. Maybe Harper could crawl out the door before the other two knew she was gone. Rick tried to tell everyone that the blackout had been part of his plan, but she could see it in his eyes that he'd been shaken to his core. She hadn't pressed him about it.

"I can't accept that is what you want to eat," Raisa said as she went back to the food simulator. "I have plenty of other recipes I can try."

Viktor tugged on Harper's arm to get her attention. He gave her a meaningful look before glancing at Raisa. Under his breath, he said, "Let her feed you."

"What?" Raisa called.

"Tasty bacon," Viktor said.

"Thanks." Raisa rapidly pushed buttons as she programmed food items into the unit.

"She needs the distraction," he whispered.

Harper finally understood why Viktor had brought her here. She sometimes forgot that not everyone was used to facing life-or-death situations. Raisa was sweet, smart, and funny, but she lacked the harder edge of people who'd seen too much. It didn't mean she wasn't capable, just that she wasn't jaded. "This might be a long shot, but do you have the code for the flat meat-bread that they make in the Ven-5 market? I was there once and bought some from a dock vendor."

Raisa smiled, nodding in excitement at the request. She clapped her hands a few times. "Yes! I can do that."

Viktor winked at Harper and nodded.

"Oh, bacon." Rick came toward the table, reaching for the plate.

"You eat that, and I won't kiss you later," Harper warned.

He instantly whipped his hand back without touching it.

"No bacon. Bad bacon. Hate bacon." Rick grabbed her hip and pulled her to him. He planted a kiss on her mouth and murmured against her lips, "Good Harper. Like Harper."

"More for me," Viktor said. The words were followed by the sound of a sliding plate.

"Here you go. Try this," Raisa said.

Harper moved to take her seat as the woman put a rolled piece of meat-bread on the table. Raisa watched her expectantly. Harper took a bite, making a point to smile and nod as she ate. The food tasted remarkably like the non-simulator variety.

Raisa pointed at her and grinned. "Now that I know what flavor profiles you like I'm going to feed you more things than you ever imagined." She turned to Rick. "And for you?"

"I'll have the same." Rick leaned next to her and whispered, "I don't want to risk not being able to kiss you later."

"Well, that's not much of a food challenge," Raisa grumbled as she went to program a second serving.

Harper chuckled and bumped his cheek playfully with the tip of her nose as she chewed. When she swallowed, she asked, "I'm curious. How did you all find each other?"

"Long story," Rick said.

"Not for me. I was buried alive by thieves, clawed my way out, went to retrieve my molecular gastro-spectrometer, didn't go well, Jackson helped me, and I've lived on the ship ever since." Raisa brought the second meat-bread to Rick before sitting with them at the table. She didn't eat. "The way I heard it, Violette tried to kidnap Dev and they fell in love. Alexis snuck on board when the crew was shopping at the Pleasure Droid warehouse."

"Not sneak. She followed Rick," Viktor corrected. "He thought she was a droid and was in love with him."

Harper arched a brow.

"My brother and I were in the process of being hung by corrupt law enforcement on Senthianick,"

Viktor answered. "Sam captained the crew back then and saved us. Dev was being crucified on an Old Earth settlement on a Data Moon Base. Jackson and Lochlann were part of a crew run by Sam's brother-by-marriage. It just happened that we all had the same purpose."

"And you?" she looked expectantly at Rick.

Rick took a big bite of food to keep from answering.

"Rick was a sad case, all lost and lonely. We took pity on him and let him join," Viktor said, smirking.

Rick made a noise of protest and swallowed. "Hardly. You begged me to join up with you."

"No. Don't recall that." Viktor took another piece of bacon.

"I had a run-in with the Medical Mafia. They wanted a cut of my salvage load, I didn't want to share, they sent a contract killer after me. I had the upper hand when Sam and these misfits showed up, and next thing I know, I'm abandoning the load and saving their asses."

"You were barely moving when you were brought on this ship. The contractor beat you nearly to death. If not for Sam, you would have died in a mud puddle," Viktor corrected.

"She sounds like a special woman," Harper said.

"Oh, don't worry, Rick isn't in love with her anymore," Viktor said.

"Shut your black hole." Rick tore a piece of meat-bread and threw it at his crewmate. To Harper, he explained, "I was never *in* love with Sam. She risked her life for us when she didn't have to. Without her, we might not have lived. She showed us we could have a purpose."

Harper couldn't help the small pang of jealousy that she felt seeing the way the men spoke of their old captain. There was a reverence in their tone. Sam was the source of their current philosophies. She was the reason they didn't think twice about saving a group of people they had never met.

"I would like to meet her," Harper said. "She sounds like an amazing woman."

"She is," Viktor agreed.

For a moment, she'd convinced herself her place on this ship was real, but the truth was she did not belong here. She was an HIA agent. If they survived this, she would go on to another mission. Rick would do his space pirate thing. Their paths should never have crossed in the first place. There was no foreseeable future for them.

That didn't mean she didn't wish there was a way for them to be together. Her chest hurt, and she had a hard time swallowing. Realizing the three of them looked at her expectantly, as if waiting for a reaction to what they had told her, she said, "Thank you for the meat-bread, Raisa."

"Do you want another?" Raisa began to stand.

Harper hadn't finished the portion she'd been given and shook her head. "No, thank you. This is perfect."

"Do I smell bacon?" Alexis appeared in the doorway with Violette.

The women entered, distracting the attention from Harper.

Seeing Rick, they paused and then shared a look.

"What?" he asked over a mouthful of food.

"We were coming to find you," Alexis said.

He swallowed and moved to stand. "Is the Ingeniarian ship back?"

"No," Violette assured him. "I think we lost them. Your artificial nebula flyby stunt worked."

He settled back into his seat.

"We need to talk to you." Alexis sat down across from them next to Raisa.

Rick leaned back and placed his hand on Harper's thigh under the table. A small tingle ran along her leg at the caress.

"It's about the ship," Violette added.

"What did you do to my girl?" He frowned. His fingers tightened on her leg. "You broke something, didn't you? Blast it, Vi, I told you to stop poking around at the controls. My lady needs a special kind of touch."

"I'm still not sure if I'm supposed to be jealous," Harper said toward Raisa as the other three were having a conversation.

Raisa chuckled.

"No, you're my lady-lady," Rick assured Harper. "She's my ship-lady."

"That doesn't comfort me." Harper laughed.

"Rick, you're a space cadet." Viktor slapped at Alexis' hand when she tried to steal a piece of bacon from his plate. Raisa instantly stood and went to the food simulator.

"What about my ship?" Rick insisted, his fingers working up her leg before snaking across her back to curl around her hip. He inched her closer to him. Harper felt his concern translated in his touch even though his tone was easygoing.

"Oh, hey, Vik." Violette pointed at his face and then swiped at her cheek as if to tell him something was on his face. When he automatically reached up to rub his cheek, Alexis swiped two pieces of bacon and passed one to Violette.

"Oh, come on, ladies, that's mine," Viktor protested.

Raisa appeared with a fresh batch, and he instantly grabbed a handful and dropped it on his plate to more than replace what was stolen.

"What about my ship?" Rick said louder.

"We need to—" Violette shoved the bacon into her mouth.

Rick leaned forward and stared at her.

Violette swallowed. "We need to destroy the ship."

Rick started to laugh, but it was a strangled sound as he realized they were serious. "What? No. You're not touching this ship."

"Technically, we're all touching the ship," Viktor said.

Rick slashed his hand in the man's direction to shut him up while keeping his attention on Alexis and Violette.

"I think I've figured out a way to create a modified version of old electromagnetic technology that would send out a pulse big enough to disrupt all side stitches and Ingeniarian security in and near the factory. It should also take out any of the bionics on the guards, at least damage their cyborg halves. That doesn't mean they won't have the ability to fight, but it would level the playing field. This also includes any communication feeds sent to the second planet." Alexis grabbed another piece of bacon. "It's our best chance."

"And you're worried about the ship?" Rick waves his hand as if dismissing the concern. "Jackson, Dev, Lochlann, and I can set the charge. The rest of you can take the ship up into orbit, where it will be safe until we're done."

"It's not that simple," Violette said.

"I'm not staying on the ship while you all fight my fight," Harper protested. "This is my mission. Freeing the workers on Ingeniare Three might not be exactly what the HIA had in mind, but they won't care as long as I disrupt the Ingeniarian's power growth. We have agents in place who will automatically ensure the damage stays done. They might not know what's happening, but they'll take any opportunity they see. So, I'll set off the pulse. You all stay on the ship until it's done. Then we'll load as many people as we can cram on board and get the hell out of there."

"You don't understand," Alexis said. "This ship would be the source of the pulse. It would be the first thing fried."

"You want to blow up our ship, our home?" Rick ran his hand over the table as if petting a living thing.

"Not blow up, more destroy as in fry every system and leave it as a hulk of useless metal," Violette said. "If we do this, this ship is not getting off the planet, not unless some hauler comes to scavenge it."

"What about the idea to give them something to

stop the bleeding?" Rick asked. "Then we wouldn't have to pulse anything.

"As I mentioned before, they mostly eat nutrient paste," Raisa said. Then glancing at Harper, she added, "Not that there is anything wrong with that, it just helps paint the picture of the conditions. We'd have to spike an entire shipment and hope it gets to all the people in the doses we'd need. That could take years depending on when they receive shipments."

"Wait," Viktor interrupted. "If we take out everything on Ingeniare Three, and we disable our ship, you're basically saying we could end up trapped on-world?"

Violette and Alexis nodded. Raisa ran her hand through her hair and bowed her head.

"It's a work in progress," Alexis said.

"What's the point of freeing the population if we can't rescue the population once they're freed? Do you expect everyone to hide on the planet?" Viktor frowned. "How long do you think it will take for the Ingeniarian government to hunt them down and reactivate the side stitches?"

"That might happen," Violette admitted, "but I think the point is we have to try."

"All I know is, if it were me, I'd want the chance." Harper didn't like this plan in its current state but trying something was better than nothing.

If they'd been talking about her parents, if there had been a chance to save them, she'd have wanted someone to try. "If they're purged, the workers are dead, anyway. At least this way they have a chance."

"What about you?" Rick gave Alexis a pointed stared. "If it shuts down everything you say it will, what about your nanoids? You can't live without them. We tried that before."

"Most of those are already inactive," Alexis answered. "I think I might have that figured out."

"Might have? How about you tell us what you *do* have figured out? Because if you dying is part of this plan, then we need a new plan. Period." Rick placed his hands on the table and stared her down.

Alexis nodded. "We have an empty scavenged radioactive holding container we can use. The protective box will be big enough to hold a few comms and lights when the pulse goes off but not much else. It's not radioactive, but it should work for our purposes. If we put the power source we took from the tracker inside with the comms, that one source should be enough to reactivate anyone who might have my unique issues—not that I expect there will be. I'm also devising something I can wear to protect me. We have all those scavenged ESC crates from Sintaz."

Rick looked around at the mess hall for a long moment before saying. "The ship doesn't matter compared to what's at stake. Let's do it. This is more plan than we've had going into most situations. The universes haven't killed us yet. We'll figure out the rest of the details when we land."

"And when the other two planets figure out what's going on? Then what?" Viktor asked. "Do we at least have a plan for that?"

"With any luck, we'll find enough supplies outside of the pulsed dead zone to repair the ship to minimum function at least long enough to get as many people as we can off-world and someplace else." Alexis didn't appear convinced by her own words.

"We were hoping maybe Harper could help us figure out something. If agents are already in place, maybe they can make sure what we are doing remains hidden, or at least buy us some time." Violette looked at her expectantly. "Or maybe even get someone to send a ride to pick us up? We could hide with the workers and pretend to be new arrivals getting ready to be fitted with a side stitch. If we're prisoners, there is no reason why we would know what's happening. That way the HIA won't have a reason to consider us a threat."

Harper shook her head. This was too damned risky. "We might be able to convince the HIA you had nothing to do with it, but if not the newcomers, then who?"

"What if we say one of the guards betrayed them?" Lucien suggested.

This plan was built around long shots and wishful thinking. They'd need more than skill to make this work, they'd need pure luck.

"I can't ask any of you to do this," Harper said. "If you're willing to sacrifice the ship, I'll fly it in and set it off. I can drop you somewhere along the way, and you can go about your lives."

They all turned to her and stared as if that was the stupidest thing they'd ever heard.

"I'm going to forget you said that," Violette said.

"No," Raisa answered at the same time. "We're doing this."

"Yeah, not happening," Alexis added. "Too much could go wrong. You can't fly the ship, and set off the modified EMP, and fight all the guards who will surely not be happy at an alien invasion. Even if you can normally maneuver a ship like this, it will be impossible between all of Rick's modifications and the systems we had to rig with spare parts done to it over the years. There's no way I can teach you all the alien technology you will need to know in case something goes wrong with the pulse. I have the files in my head. I need to be there when it happens, and I need Raisa and Viktor helping me. We'll have to connect it to the ship after we land. It's too dangerous to do while we're flying. Lucien will keep track of everyone and relay orders. Jackson, Lochlann, Dev, and Rick will handle any guards left standing after the pulse. Everyone will help with crowd control. There is sure to be confusion and panic amongst the workers."

"I'll help with the guards," Violette said. "Blasters will be down so it'll be hand-to-hand combat."

"I think there may be something in the Hungariz lab we can use to help subdue the guards," Alexis said, "and help any locals who may have a reaction to the side stitch deactivating. With instant shut off, it shouldn't release any blood thinners because we're not pulling them out. It's a low-tech solution but there are manual injectors in the lab."

"I can show you how they work if any of you hasn't used them before," Harper offered.

Rick grunted. "Yeah, she has no problem using injectors."

Harper hit him lightly on the leg. He winked at her.

"I'll go with the forward team," Harper said, knowing she should be on the frontline of the fight. "I can try to get a message to the agents on Ingeniare Two and let them know I'm with cleared HIA assets, but I'm not sure I'll hear back from them by the time we arrive. With a great amount of luck, they'll be able to arrange to have someone help with the relocation. Even on the very remote chance we get a ship to transport the population from the planet, I can't guarantee what will happen to this crew if someone decided to check on your asset status because you're not going to be cleared in the system. We can try to hide some of you with the population and smuggle you out."

"We've had worse odds," Violette said.

"When?" Lucien asked.

"Any time Rick gets behind the flight controls," she answered.

Rick ignored her teasing. "And what is our excuse to get close enough to do this? Or are we going in hot?"

"Still working on that part. I think there is a landing pad we can use to put us in the right posi-tion," Alexis answered.

"I'm sure you can come up with a quick excuse to talk our way in, Rick," Violette said.

Rick nodded. He pushed up from the table and held his hand out to Harper. "If you need us, I'll be kissing Harper in our quarters."

Harper slipped her hand into his and let him lead her from the mess hall. To Raisa, she said, "Thanks again for the food."

Raisa gave a small wave.

As she turned the corner, she heard Raisa say, "I think I'm going to track down Jackson."

"If you need me, I'll be with Dev in the cargo hold," Violette said.

"Yeah, I think Lochlann was taking a nap. I'm going to join him," Alexis said.

"Viktor, you need anything?" Raisa asked.

"I'm going to be right here with all the bacon," he answered. "My sweet, sweet bacon."

Rick ran his hand along the corridor wall, tracing the soft glow of light that shone from behind its clear casing. "I know this ship doesn't look like much—she's old and starting to rust, her insides are cobbled together from scavenged parts, and we had a blood-drinking monster hidden in the walls for years without knowing it. This was my first home. After Sam and the guys saved me, this is where we became a family. I know every inch of this ship, all her secrets and her quirks. She saved our lives more than a few times." A small laugh escaped him. "And she almost killed us a few times, too."

Harper stopped walking and watched his back. He took several steps before realizing she wasn't following. When he turned to face her, she said, "I have to ask again if you're sure. This is your home. You love this ship. I can find another way to help—"

"You need to let me finish. As much as I love the freedom this ship represents, it's only metal and wires. What matters are the people she carries. We'll find another ship someday." Rick tapped the wall thoughtfully with the pads of his fingers. "From the very first rivet, this ship was destined for adventure —not some boring cargo freighter or transporter. I can think of no better end for her run than to help free those trapped on Ingeniare Three. There is no choice to make. *The Bound Virgin* is meeting her end, and she's going out in true pirate style."

The feeling of Harper against Rick's skin lingered even when she wasn't near him. It remained pressed between his flesh and clothes, embedded on his nerves, and twisted into his soul. He now understood what he could have lost with the curse, what he still might lose. To those looking in, four happy couples out of five would still be considered a great success in breaking a curse, but not if you were the one left standing heartbroken.

They had all faced impossible odds before. They'd been chased by the Federation Military, the Larceny Casino, the Medical Mafia, Dokka traders, criminals and lawmen, and more corporations than he'd bothered to count. They'd escaped capture and death. They'd been strung up, shot up, tied up, beat up, and blown up. They'd nearly run out of oxygen in the deep black. They'd crash-landed a spaceship in a Qurilixen field.

They were pirates. They accepted this was how pirates lived.

They were not ready for death.

Rick was not ready for death. Not anymore. Not since Harper.

For years he'd lived for one very simple reason—to keep his crew safe while they flew the high skies trying to do good. Family gave him purpose. Now, selfishly, he wanted to live for himself. He wanted more time with Harper. He wanted to wake up for the next eternity in her arms. He wanted to explore every single piece of dirt and metal the universes had to offer—with her. He wanted...

Rick took a deep breath.

He just wanted her.

"Rick?" Harper whispered. "Are you going to answer them?"

His hands trembled as they hovered over the controls. Violette sat next to him in the copilot seat. Harper had arrived as they neared the surface and stood beside him. The rest of the crew were in position, ready for the attack.

Ingeniare Three had grown large in the viewing screen. Even from the air, it looked to be a terrible place. The barren landscape was not fit for inhabitants as if someone smudged a layer of dust and sheered metal particles over the sky. His lungs hurt just looking at it. The only sign of life on the other-wise dead planet was the factory. The air was a little clearer above the metal structure as if they ran vent ships to clear the choked atmosphere.

It wasn't too late to whip the ship around and head toward the nearest fueling dock. If he over-rode Violette's controls, he could have them out of there before anyone could stop him. It was the only way to ensure they all remained safe.

"This is Ingeniare Three ground. Identify your purpose," the voice on the comm repeated.

Harper slid her hand onto his shoulder. She reached for the comm button as if to do it herself.

Rick beat her to it, pushing the button to answer, "Delivery."

That one gruff word was all Rick could manage. There was a long pause. Harper and Violette looked at him questioningly.

"We pay six for male prisoners, four for females, won't take them if they're pregnant, sick, missing their hands, or defective," the voice answered. "Head to the center dock."

Harper sighed with relief.

"I don't know what I find most offensive about this situation," Violette said from the copilot seat as she prepared the ship for landing.

Harper leaned over to kiss him. She held his cheek and smiled. "I'll see you after we land."

"Don't leave until I get there," Rick said.

"I'll do what I have to." She kissed him again before hurrying out of the cockpit. He heard her running toward the cargo hold.

"I like her," Violette said. "Well done."

Rick forced an unconcerned smile even as his heart beat a little too heavily. He stared at the factory as they steered the ship closer. Hitting the ship comms, he said, "Buckle in. This atmosphere looks rough."

"Hey." Violette's hand slid over his as she leaned toward him from her chair. Her eyes met his. "Harper is trained for this. We're all going to get through this alive. I know it. This is not how we meet our ends."

He wasn't sure who she was trying to convince.

Rick nodded. "You know, I don't think I've ever told you that you're not a half bad pilot. Not as good as me, but not half bad."

Violette slapped his hand before leaning back. "There he is. The spacehole we know and love."

"Don't tell Dev you're in love with me," Rick warned, trying to distract his nervousness with banter.

"I'm more worried about Harper. I see the way

she looks at you. If she's not in love, I don't know who would be."

Rick couldn't help the grin her words caused.

"She hasn't said it, has she?"

Rick didn't answer but his smile fell.

Violette waved her hand as if the detail wasn't important. "I wouldn't read too much into that fact. I think it's harder for women like us. So many alien species treat women like they're delicate. I think it has something to do with our carrying children that makes most males protective. So when we are raised in a strict environment filled with men—*tough men*— we feel we have to prove something, that we're not emotional and that we're as tough as any of them." Violette pulled up her sleeve to show the long, ugly scar on her forearm. "This was how my father showed his love. Harper's parents showed it by sending her away to fend for herself."

The ship began to shake as they broke through the atmosphere.

"Make sure you tell her how you feel," Violette instructed. "Use the words."

"I have," Rick assured her. "I do."

"Then keep showing her." Violette grunted as they were tossed up against their belts. "Trust her to do what she needs to do. We only get one chance at something great. Harper is yours."

"Are you sure you want to do this?" Lochlann held the electric cuffs in his hands but made no move to put them on Harper's outstretched wrists. Dev was already cuffed and waiting by the cargo bay door. Jackson stood with him, playing the part of the captor. Rick and Violette had yet to join them from the cockpit.

"Are you sure you want to be in here?" Harper returned. "If you want to be with your wife…?"

"Of course I'd rather be with my wife, but if she says she can do this, I trust her," Lochlann said. The words were brave, but he didn't try to hide his worry. It would seem the men on this ship only knew one way to love—completely. He lifted the cuffs and repeated the question she avoided. "Are *you* sure? This will leave you more vulnerable."

"Once they set off the pulse, the current will be disrupted and they should unlatch," Harper said. "Rick told them you were selling prisoners. So, we need to sell prisoners. If anyone recognizes me as Eloise, Prince Bucky's fiancée, they'll let you in. Either they know he is looking for me, or they'll wonder why I'm unescorted."

"And probably kill us for having captured you," Lochlann said. "It makes more sense to have you with us, commanding us."

"Unless Bucky or his gossiping bodyguards made it known that I betrayed him. No, they'll be too confused as they try to find answers. We just need to buy enough time for Alexis to set off the pulse." Harper slipped her hand into the cuffs and waited for Lochlann to close them. He hesitated a second before pressing them together.

The feel of cold metal against her skin caused a small shiver to roll over her. She did not like the sensation of being trapped, but she'd trained for combat many times with bound hands. Aside from Jackson, and maybe Dev, none of the other appeared to have much in the way of formal combat training. There was a vast difference between an all-out brawl and going up against trained guards. Harper had not fought beside any of the pirates but Rick, and the unknown factor as to how they would react made this mission all the more dangerous. At least with HIA, they were all trained relatively the same and could read each other's signals.

Harper knew if the guards seized anyone, it would be the prisoners first. That put her on the frontline. Dev was an obvious choice for co-prisoner as he would be a great prize to any labor facility masquerading as a legitimate factory. The sad part was most people didn't care what happened here so long as they were able to play with their neat bionic toys.

Harper tried not to think of Rick but it was impossible. She wished him trapped in the cockpit, imagined that Alexis set the pulse off too soon and he couldn't get out. He'd be safe there until they managed to pry the door open.

"Don't forget, if you get the chance, sever the tubes at the back of their arms if the armor isn't in the way," Harper said of the guards' bionic limbs. "It's their most vulnerable location."

It was also one of the hardest locations to get to in a fight. Normally, if you were close enough to sever the tubes, you were about to be punched to death.

"It shouldn't come to that. The pulse should disable their bionic limbs," Lochlann answered.

A loud bang sounded on the outside wall, causing her breath to catch.

Harper nodded to Lochlann that she was ready. The captain's eyes yellowed with a bioluminescent glow. His flesh tightened, hardening to a dark brown shell. His forehead widened as a ridge grew down the center to create an armor over his nose and brow. Talons formed from the tips of his thickened fingers. When he opened his mouth to draw in a deep breath, fangs peaked from beneath his lips. It only took seconds for him to change into the form of a walking dragon.

Lochlann swiped his taloned hand over the scanner to open the cargo bay door. The loud creak of metal sounded over the silent cargo hold. No one spoke. They didn't have to. The stress of anticipation was thick in the air, revealed in the stiffness of stances and the narrowing of eyes.

Bright light flooded the cargo, covering their feet and slowly moving up their bodies as the door opened. Lochlann grabbed the back of her arm. His grip was firm but didn't cause her pain.

She braced herself for an army of bio-guards.

The door lifted, and she blinked against the light to adjust her eyes. A slender humanoid man with an electronic clipboard stood before them. His arms glowed to show he was fitted with bionic parts, but even that didn't make him appear to be an opposing figure. His eyes were large and placed closely together on his face.

Harper leaned her head forward to glance around the loading dock. A few guards loitered by the door. One yawned and the other one fussed with a bio-tube on his arm. Two workers in tattered clothing pushed a supply cart along the edge of the landing pad. They glanced at the ship but did not stop in their task.

So much for the great army.

"Welcome to Ingeniare Three. I'm Varin, and I will be assisting you today," the slender man said, his voice a bored drawl. He glanced up but hardly appeared concerned by the scene before him. "How many on board today?"

"Two," Lochlann answered, the gravelly tone to his shifted voice coming out brusque.

The intake guard frowned and made a big show of sighing in exasperation. "How many on board the ship?"

"Two prisoners," Lochlann repeated. If Harper had been on the other side of that gruff voice, it would've sent a shiver a fear over her. The intake guard looked jaded enough to have seen it all before.

"Never mind, we'll scan the ship," Varin answered. He took a writing device and drew on the clipboard. "Two prisoners." He glanced up. "One female. One male. Any cargo to trade?"

"No," Lochlann answered.

"Bring the woman forward," Varin ordered. Lochlann's grip tightened slightly as he walked her out of the ship. Jackson and Dev began to move as well, but the intake guard lifted his hand to stop them. "Just the female."

Varin pulled a scanner off his belt and lifted it toward Harper. He drew it over her body, starting at her head and working down to her feet. The man stared at his clipboard a few seconds before saying, "Sorry, we can't take that one. You might try Ingeniare Two. Bring down the male."

Harper frowned. What did he mean he wasn't going to take her? If this wasn't a prisoner intake, his dismissal of her would have been highly insulting.

"Why?" Lochlann demanded, and Harper assumed he was buying as much time as he could. "She's a good female."

Yeah, I'm a good female, Harper thought, curious to know the answer herself.

"She's defective," Varin dismissed. "Bring the male."

Defective? Harper would show this black hole defective.

Lochlann's grip tightened on her arm and he drew her closer to his side as if to stop her from making a scene.

This time Varin ran the scanner over Dev but

didn't look at the results. "We can use him." He turned to yell over his shoulder. "I need one side stitch."

"How much?" Lochlann moved her closer to where Dev and Jackson stood.

"We pay six thousand space credits for the males," the man said.

"I want eight," Lochlann argued. "He can do the work of many."

Varin again looked annoyed. He eyed Dev, then the scan he took, before saying, "Fine. We can do eight. We don't get many with Bevlon blood here. If you run across anymore, bring them."

Dev growled at Varin. The intake guard had enough sense to step back.

"Do you need his prisoner documents?" Jackson asked.

Varin laughed and shook his head in denial as he turned his back on them. Another worker appeared, pushing a hover cart toward them covered with a gray cloth. The circular pattern of the side stitch showed through the man's threadbare clothing. His eyes were blank as he stared at the floor. Scars slashed his hands and arms and would undoubtedly continue along the rest of his body.

Varin pulled the cloth back and took hold of an inactive side stitch. "Lift his shirt."

Dev growled again.

"Do you need assistance with him?" Varin asked when Jackson didn't do as he was told.

Lochlann nodded toward Jackson who then lifted Dev's shirt to expose his side. Dev tried to shake the man off. Somehow Dev ended up kneeling on the floor with Jackson pressing into him.

"Keep him steady," Varin ordered.

Jackson stared at the man, not moving.

Varin held the side stitch between his fingers as he approached Dev. The device's claws extended like sharp little knives. "Don't worry, you'll learn to behave soon enough."

"I'd say it's time," Rick's voice boomed behind her, signaling to the team it was time to detonate. So much for him being trapped in the safety of the cockpit.

"Time?" Varin blinked.

That moment of hesitation was enough of a distraction. Jackson released his friend. Dev growled and surged to his feet, shoving his elbow upward to knock Varin's hand. The side stitch flew upward and embedded into the soft tissue beneath Varin's chin. He screamed as the device dug its way into his face and then flailed on the floor as he tried to pull it out. He screamed again, and Harper saw the tips of the claws piercing through to the man's mouth as they searched for a place to anchor.

Rick joined them near the opening.

Violette rushed from the back to Lochlann. "They're close but Alexis needs more time. They ran into a problem rerouting the power from the ship's circuit. We have to hold them off."

At the commotion, an alarm sounded, blaring over the facility. The side-stitched worker with the hover cart backed away from the scene, not running but definitely not helping. Guards filtered in from each of the doors, charging toward the ship.

And there's the army, Harper thought as she braced herself for a fight.

She gave the worker a pointed look and yelled, "Hide."

To her surprise, he ran into the ship. "Take me with you."

Lochlann shoved him into the protective cubby between two crates.

"What the hell is this?" Rick demanded as he joined her side to see she was cuffed. He gripped several emergency flares in his hand labeled with the logo for the Exploratory Science Commission.

"Catch," Lochlann ordered, tossing them each a blaster pistol. She caught it but the design of the cuffs made it challenging to hold the weapon with both hands. She let her left hand dangle as she aimed with her right.

Shots pinged the metal opening. Rick pulled her behind the safety of a cargo container. More shots reverberated. Harper poked her head up and fired back. She saw a couple of downed bio-guards on the floor. Their buddies stepped over them, not bothering to check if they were alive.

Rick leaned around the side of the container to do the same. More shots answered theirs. They were definitely outnumbered.

"Blast it," Jackson swore.

"Are you hit?" Lochlann called.

Jackson grunted. "I'm fine."

A high-pitched whine came from within their ship. Harper peeked up before ducking to safety. The sound was enough to make the guards stumble in their progress toward them.

"Here we go," Rick whispered.

Harper flinched as the sound became almost unbearable. She pressed an ear to her shoulder while holding her hand against the other one.

Eeeeeeeeeeee—POOF.

The sound crescendoed into that of all technological devices shutting off at the same time, with only the faint residual hum of dying engines. Harper lowered her hands. The cuffs fell from her and clanked on the floor. She heard Dev's do the same. The loading dock lights turned off, leaving the gray daylight from above to cast shadows over the area. The guards fell to the floor as their bionic limbs stopped working.

A stunned laughed escaped Violette.

"Holy space balls, it worked," Jackson exclaimed in surprise.

Rick led the way from behind the crates. He pulled the trigger on his blaster but the weapon was dead. He set it on a container.

A combination of murmurs and angry shouts came from the downed guards. A few of them began pushing to their feet.

Lochlann pulled out a metal container and opened it. A handful of comms, small lights, and Harper's broken side stitch were within. He tapped one of the comms. It made a popping sound. "I think they're working."

He tossed a couple at Dev and Jackson. They weren't as lucky with the lights. Lochlann tried turning them on only to find they were dead. He tossed them aside.

"Start cutting," Lochlann ordered.

Dev and Jackson slapped the comms onto their shoulders and pulled knives from their boots. They went toward the nearest guards. Though lacking bio strength, the guards were still able to put up a fight.

"Alexis." Lochlann set the comms down and took the power source as he ran into the ship to check on his wife.

Rick hit the end of a flare and threw it across the loading docks into a dark corner. A red glow filled the area, outlining the men on the floor. He shoved the remaining flares in his waistband.

Violette went to the worker hiding between the crates. "Stand up. Let me see your side."

Harper didn't wait. She grabbed the knife she'd hid near the cargo door and grabbed a comm from the box Lochlann had left behind. She felt Rick right behind her.

"We need to incapacitate as many as we can in case any of them find a way to reactivate," Harper said. Cutting the tubes wouldn't kill them, but it would make them about as harmless as an angry toddler. Though, considering some alien toddlers were scary as hell, that wasn't exactly the most comforting of thoughts.

Dev and Jackson went up against those who had enough natural muscle mass left after their procedures to still fight. Jackson took a blow to the face, his head snapping back before he righted himself. He gave a fierce yell as he grabbed hold of his opponent and lifted him into the air. With a mighty heft, he threw the guard into three of his comrades knocking them over.

Dev slammed two heads together, knocking them unconscious. Lochlann appeared next to Dev. It was impossible to read his expression while in dragon-man form. He nodded once at her questioning look to indicate Alexis survived as he rejoined the fight.

"Alexis is fine," Harper told Rick. He let go of a long sigh.

Harper went toward the bio-guards who were still on the ground. They'd been dependent on the bio-fluid longer and their natural muscles had weakened, making it difficult to stand. Even injured they were dangerous. They crawled toward her, trying to grab her ankles and pull her down. What they lacked in super strength they made up for in sheer numbers. Two she could fight. Twenty would pull her under a sea of smothering, angry bodies. She kept moving, kicking and shoving, as she grabbed their damaged arms and severed the tubes. Green bio-fluid spurted from them, and she tried not to let it coat her clothing. It created slippery pools on the floor.

Rick stayed close to do the same. A woman snarled at him as he cut her arm tubes, and she tried to grab hold as if to bite. Harper kicked at her side and sent her sliding away.

"It worked. This guy's side stitch is still attached but deactivated," Violette yelled.

Harper looked up at the sound. One of the fallen guards grabbed her foot and yanked hard. She fell, nearly stabbing herself with the blade as she slammed into the floor. Fingers gripped her hair and pulled. Bodies rolled over her, trapping her down with their weight. Harper kicked and punched as she tried to throw them off her.

"Harper," Rick yelled. She felt the weight being lifted from her stomach. Being as she was at the wrong angle to stab, Harper punched with her knife hand at the man trapping her head. She swung several times, hitting his hip and groin. He groaned as her knuckles made contact with his balls. He let go of her hair, and she was able to swing her body upright.

The man moaned in pain as he cupped himself. Harper sliced the tubes along the back of his arms. Rick hooked her beneath her arm and pulled her to her feet. The bio-fluid coated her clothing.

Viktor appeared from inside the ship with a pack slung over his shoulder. "Lucien and I are securing the communications tower."

Lucien rushed ahead of his brother, leading through an open path between the fallen guards.

"Rick, Harper, come on. I've got the med kits." Raisa leaped over a leg as a guard tried to trip her.

"They look like a bunch of sunbathing fish on the beach," Alexis observed. She shoved one aside with her foot to send him sliding. Dark circles had formed under her eyes, and her face was pale and splotched with red, indicating that whatever she'd gone through when the pulse went off had most likely been painful.

"Careful, they still bite," Harper answered.

"Our new friend says the factory floor is through here." Violette jogged past them toward an opened door.

"Lochlann, you got this?" Rick yelled instead of using a comm.

"Go!" Lochlann ran after one of the guards trying to lunge at Alexis and dove on top of him. The dragon-man knocked him over. Lochlann punched him several times as they both slid. Dev and Jackson faced off against four of the remaining guards who had made it to their feet.

Following Violette toward one of the doors, Rick placed a hand on Harper's shoulder before they went inside. The angry shouts of the fallen guards had lessened. He eyed her in concern. His thumb moved across her cheek, wiping a droplet of bio-fluid that must have splashed there. "You injured?"

"I'm good." Harper glanced over him as she rubbed her arms and wrung her hair. The sound of bio-fluid droplets rained on the floor. "You?"

"Good." Rick nodded.

He grabbed her hand as they left the loading docks. They entered a dark corridor. She didn't need him to guide her but felt comfort in his touch.

"It's too quiet," Violette whispered. "I expected there to be chaos."

Harper frowned. She quickened her pace as they neared a door with a series of Ingeniarian symbols. "Here."

She slowly pushed the door open and eased her way inside. There were only a few narrow windows along the perimeter. Rick appeared next to her with a flare. He threw it to the side. The red light revealed rows of production equipment.

Workers stood before each machine as if they hadn't dared to move when the equipment stopped running. Eyes turned toward them, embedded in tired faces. They looked underfed, which was a hard thing to do if they were on a diet of nutrient paste. Several appeared frightened and drew their arms closer to their bodies as if to appear smaller. They turned their eyes toward the ground and leaned into the machines.

Harper walked along the perimeter of the room, peering down the perfectly spaced aisles. Light tapping noises came from somewhere near the back.

"There are hundreds of them," Raisa whispered. "What's wrong with them? Why aren't they moving?"

"They're frightened," Harper said. "They're probably threatened if they leave their posts without permission."

"I'm never using biotech again," Raisa swore. "We need to show this to everyone. They can't get away with this."

"Greetings." Alexis cautiously approached a woman. "My name is Alexis. These are my friends. We're here to help. Do you speak the Old Star language?"

Harper went to a man standing by a drill with a bit twice his size. She pointed toward his side. "Show me?"

The man didn't move. Harper kept an eye on his face as she reached to lift his tunic. She gently touched the side stitch. The lights were not blinking and the unit didn't appear to be giving off a vibration.

"This stitch is deactivated," Harper said, dropping the shirt and moving to the next one. She gestured to a man with reptilian skin. "Can I see it? Will you come closer to the light?"

"They'll kill us," the man whispered, his teeth clenched. "We can't leave our stations."

"These are dead over here, too," Violette called.

The man stiffened and his eyes widened. He moved closer to his machine.

"No, she means the side stitches. Not people." Harper tried to reach for his shirt to show him but he slapped her hand away. Harper took a step back to show she meant no harm. "No problem, I won't touch. Just make sure it's not on and you're not bleeding. We're only here to help."

"We're here to help," Rick repeated, loudly. He lit another flare and threw it down the aisle. More faces were revealed from the darkness. "Who's in charge?"

A woman stared at him and lifted her hand while keeping it close to her body. When Rick started toward her, she pointed upward.

"I'll take care of the bosses." Violette touched the comm on her shoulder. "Dev, we need you. Factory floor. Upper left quadrant."

Seconds later, Dev appeared with Jackson. Violette pointed to where the woman indicated. Jackson picked up one of the flares and used it like a torch to light their way.

A hairy beast of a man lifted his shirt without having to be asked. Lykan males did not scare easily, and the fact he still stood by his post said more than words could. "They'll detonate these if we try to leave."

Rick put himself between her and the Lykan. The protective gesture appeared to be an automatic reflex, but it wasn't needed.

The sound of something dropping stopped them from answering.

"Over here!" Raisa yelled.

Harper and Rick ran toward her voice, only to

find her kneeling on the floor next to a fallen man. He moaned and kicked his legs.

"He just collapsed," Raisa said as she lifted his shirt. "The tracker is attached but bleeding."

"Hand me the injector," Harper ordered.

Raisa retrieved one from the medical kit. "There's so much blood."

"Rick, help me turn him." Harper angled the injector.

The man protested and fought as Rick rolled him onto his side. Harper shoved the injector into the man's ass cheek.

"Wrap gauze around the wound," Harper told Raisa.

Raisa pointed across the aisle. "There's another one."

Harper hurried to the woman, even as she heard two more drops.

"Give me one of those," Rick said to Raisa.

"Check your side stitches," Harper yelled to the workers. "We need to make sure you're not bleeding."

She saw a few of them look at their sides.

"Bosses neutralized," Violette's voice came over the comm, her breath a little heavy. "We have five hundred and sixty-seven workers on the floor. Twenty-three in the infirmary. We're on our way there now to check on them."

"Understood," Alexis' voice answered.

Harper motioned to a nearby worker. "What's your name?"

"Thagna." The woman didn't move.

"Come over here and help hold her steady," Harper instructed.

Thagna kneeled beside her fellow worker and placed her hands on the woman's shoulders while Harper looked at the tracker.

"Thagna, you're going to help me. We need to find anyone who might be bleeding and give them this medicine." Harper aimed the injector and pushed at her patient's hip. "Hold her still."

"We have a medical booth," Thagna said.

"In order to deactivate the trackers we had to fry all equipment in this facility," Harper explained. "There is no medical booth. No guards. No lights. Just us. We need to work fast."

She jabbed the injector into the patient's ass cheek. "After I inject them, you need to wrap their shirts gently around the stitch. We want to stop as much blood loss as we can. Once we make sure everyone is all right, we'll work on a plan to get you all out of here."

Thagna nodded.

To the woman she'd just injected, Harper said, "Try not to move around. We'll come back to check on you."

"Meger," Thagna said to a dark-haired man. "Run the lines. Have anyone who is bleeding from their tracker sit on the floor. Tell them help is coming." Then to a woman with green fur, she ordered, "Screl, gather those who are not bleeding and lead them to the dining hall."

"Looks like I picked the right woman for the job," Harper said. Thagna gave a small smile at the compliment.

"We're sending the uninjured to the dining hall," Harper said into the comm.

"I'll send a flare with them," Rick answered. She glanced to where he was down the aisle and saw him light a flare. He handed it to the man and gestured at him to go.

Harper moved from one fallen person to the next. Between each one, she glanced to find Rick. With Thagna's help, she was able to move a lot faster down the line.

"How's it looking?" Alexis' voice came over the comm.

"Only a few more on this side," Thagna said.

Harper nodded and repeated the information to the others. She stretched her back. Her injector was getting low. It had become harder to see what she was doing. They had reached the edge of the red flare light and would need to move it forward.

Rick joined her. "Harper? Did you hear that?"

"Wh—"

Rick held up his hand, silencing her. He tilted his head.

Thud. Thump. Thump.

Harper stiffened.

Thump. Thump. Thump.

"Someone is coming," Rick whispered. They heard light footsteps coming toward them from the darkness.

Thagna gasped and inched toward one of the nearby worktables. Rick motioned that Harper should follow Thagna under the table.

"Guys, is that you?" Alexis' voice on the comm sounded concerned.

As if to answer, a bright light flooded the factory as armed figures covered in black dropped from the ceiling and advanced on them. Masks hid their faces.

"The Ingeniarians know we're here," Rick said.

Thagna screamed and instantly went to the ground, covering her head as if to make herself as small as possible.

Thump. Thump.

Rick grabbed Harper's hand and tried to run toward the exit.

Thump. Thump. Thump.

Three more masked intruders dropped down to block their escape. They wore full tactical gear, including the large blasters aimed in Harper and Rick's direction. It was impossible to see if they were equipped with bio-tubes. The sound of fighting came from the other side of the factory. Dev's voice echoed over them but there was no way for them to help.

One of the intruders came forward, towering over the rest. He pulled the mask from his head. Streaks of blond slashed through his darker hair. The stark color of his green eyes caught her attention as he focused in on them. He didn't appear bionic, but even without bio-fluid he was formidable.

"I'll distract them. You run," Rick whispered.

Harper wasn't going anywhere without him.

"Agent Harper Virant?" the giant of a man asked. "You're a hard woman to track. We've been looking for you."

"Run!" Rick yelled like a wild man and tried to shove her out of the way as he charged the large warrior. Harper tried to go after him. Rick managed to get in a substantial blow before the armed men converged on him, tackling him to the ground.

Rick worked his hands against the cuffs. He glared at the giant man talking to Harper, just waiting for him to make a move that gave him the excuse he needed to charge him again. A few of the men had taken off their protective gear to reveal they weren't part of the bio-jerk army.

Harper had not been cuffed but there was a pair next to where the two stood. The bio-fluid had dried to her clothing, staining it. Her hair was a mess of plastered locks. Three guards stood behind her, staring at her back as if waiting for her to try something. The conversation was obviously tense if their expressions were any indication.

Rick sat with most of his crew, bound and gagged on the floor of the loading dock near their ship. Even if they could make it on board to escape, the ship was dead and wouldn't be flying anywhere.

Jackson's arm bled, and Dev had a large knot on the side of his head. Violette and Raisa were bound away from their husbands, which seemed to be causing the men more distress than their injuries. Lucien and Viktor had been tied together and sat back-to-back. Lochlann had it the worst, as he continually searched the loading dock for his wife. Alexis had not been seen.

Several men had been assigned the task of mopping up the bio-fluids from the loading dock. All the bio-guards had been moved.

The commander reached toward Harper. Rick struggled to get loose.

"Sit down!" A black-clad spacehole shoved Rick down by his shoulder. "I won't tell you again."

Rick gave a muffled response, basically threatening the man's ability to procreate.

Harper slapped the giant man's hand, grabbed the cuffs, and yelled, "Then you might as well hold me prisoner too because I'm not telling you a blasted thing until you let my assets go."

She marched toward Rick and sat down, dropping the cuffs by her feet. The man frowned but didn't follow her.

Rick tried to ask her what was going on, but the sound of his voice was inaudible thanks to the gag.

He wasn't the only one. The rest of them were looking at her too.

"HIA," Harper stated. "With a little Federation Military support thrown in. The man I was talking to in charge of this operation is Agent Dietrich Bauer. They were either sent to assist us or apprehend us. I don't think he's decided yet."

One of the guards eavesdropped on what she was saying. He didn't even try to hide it.

"Unfortunately, ship logs aren't accessible to verify that you're important HIA assets," Harper said, "but I would remind all of you that you're not at liberty to discuss any part of this mission, not even to the operation leader." She looked up to the eavesdropper. "They'll have to kill you first, and that will piss off some very important people. My word on the matter will have to be good enough."

Rick instantly understood that Harper was taking responsibility for their entire plan. He would have protested, but the gag stopped his words.

Lochlann made a strangled sound to get her attention. His eyes widened.

"They stowed all of your property. It's inside the ship. Even that droid," Harper said.

Lochlann closed his eyes and released a long breath as if he'd been holding it for the last hour.

"Agent Virant," Bauer's voice boomed over the docks. "Get back here."

"Release my assets," she yelled back. "You have your orders. I have mine."

He marched toward her. To the eavesdropper, he ordered, "Step back."

The man obeyed, giving them space to talk.

"I need to know why you attacked this planet." Bauer crouched in front of Harper to better look her in the eye. His tone sounded more exasperated than angry. He eyed the crew. They glared back at him.

"Release my assets." Harper drew her legs up and rested her arms on them.

"From where we stand, you went rogue. This was not part of the mission," Bauer continued.

"Release my assets," she repeated.

"You were to infiltrate Ingeniare One's royal family, not attack Ingeniare Three."

"Release my—"

"Bloody nova," Bauer swore. He motioned for the eavesdropper to return. "Untie them. But if anyone runs, shoot them."

The guard didn't appear too pleased to be letting the prisoners go. As he pulled the gag off of Rick's mouth, Rick blew him a kiss and winked. "Thanks."

When they were freed, Bauer again waved the man away.

"Let us try this again." Bauer stood, waiting for

them to do the same. "Give me one reason to believe you did not go rogue. Your mission was to infiltrate Ingeniare One, not attack Ingeniare Three. The last check-in has you heading to the VR Advanced Technology and Programming Conference on Nozando. We have confirmed you arrived at the event. Now Prince Bucky is missing, the royals are tightening security, and we find you fumbling around in the dark with people we can't verify."

"You weren't read into my mission, and I am not authorized to give you details," Harper denied. "So, you might as well stop asking."

"I was read into every part of this mission," he countered.

Bauer reached into his pocket and pulled out a device. He held it up. Harper's photo appeared next to the words "*Classified File 7890-8889.*"

Harper's expression changed, and Rick felt her stiffen. He wanted to move closer to her, but she'd made it clear they weren't to say anything, and that probably meant the nonverbal as well. It took everything inside of Rick to keep back. Agent Bauer didn't need to know that Rick and Harper were lovers. If they think she ran off with a romantic affair, that might make things worse for her.

"I brought this mission forward," Bauer said. Rick had the impression the man didn't want to detain them unless he had to during the course of his job.

"My directive was to undermine the power of the royal family." She gestured around. He could tell by the look in her eyes that she didn't think there was a way out of the situation. She was trying to put all of the blame on herself, in an attempt to save the rest of them. "You're welcome. Royal family's power undermined."

"Where is Prince Bucky?" he asked. "Did you dispose of him?"

"To the best of my knowledge, he flew himself into a nebula," Harper said. "The artificial kind, not the harmless kind. Beyond that, I don't know."

"What supposed nebula?" Bauer looked as if he wanted to believe her but couldn't.

"I don't think it had a name." Harper glanced at Rick.

Rick cleared his throat. "Harpy Nebula."

Harper's lips pressed together, and she briefly closed her eyes as if to bite back a laugh.

"Never heard of it," Bauer answered.

"I can point it out on a star chart," Violette offered. At some point, she had inched closer to her husband. Jackson had switched places with her and stood with his body blocking Raisa from the guards. Lochlann had stepped back and was peeking up into the ship's cargo hold.

"Get her a star chart and send a team to check on the prince," Bauer ordered the eavesdropper. Then to Harper, he said, "Even if what you say about Bucky is true, it does not change the fact that you are here on an unauthorized mission taking out a very valuable, powerful trio of planets. An act like this does not go unnoticed in the galaxies."

"Someone had to do it," Harper said. "If you are the one who brought this mission forward, then you know what this place is. You know what they do to people here, about the factory purges. You know these people do not belong here. They are merely pawns used for the gain of the royal family."

"I might have been read into all of the missions, but you were not. Why do you think I was trying to lessen their power?" Bauer placed a hand on Harper's shoulder and lightened his tone. "A move like this takes time. We don't need a bio-army starting an intergalactic event."

Rick pressed his lips together and stared at the agent's hand. Who did this man think he was? Frowning, he said, "A plan that slow could take decades and easily be forgotten halfway through as politics change. What about the people who are here now? They do not deserve this life or to be purged into the next one."

"Don't make me gag you again," Bauer warned.

"Rick, please, don't," Harper said, before

turning to Bauer once more. "The bio-guards are not very dangerous once they're disarmed."

"I'm going to need to know how you did that," Bauer said. "Our people have been trying for nearly a year to disarm the bionics. The best they have is cutting the tubes, which from the amount of fluid on the floor you already know."

"You can thank my assets for disarming them," Harper said. "Clear them and let them go and I'm sure they'll give you plans for the device. Then you won't have to worry about a bio-army. All the bionic Ingeniarians will be stopped before they can even utter the command to attack."

"We also need a place to relocate all of these people to." Bauer dropped his hand away and gestured to the factory. "Do you have a plan for that as well?"

"Not—" Harper began.

Suddenly, tiny lights rained down from above like noiseless sparks.

They all glanced up in surprise, though there didn't appear to be a source for the energy.

Several gasps filled the loading dock. A soft pink glow appeared amongst the darkly clothed men. As the sparks stopped falling, the glow lightened to reveal a young woman. Long brown hair fell to her waist, and she smiled as if entirely unconcerned by the fact she had materialized into a room filled with armed men. She wore an ethereal gown of pure white. It appeared to float around her as she moved. The soldiers stepped back to give the creature space.

Bauer stiffened even as his mouth opened in surprise.

"Is that a ghost?" Lucien asked.

"That almost looks like the ancestral spirits on Lintian," Jackson said.

"Rick, quick, insult her and get Lucien and I cursed to find women, too," Viktor whispered.

Rick didn't answer.

Harper touched Bauer's arm to get his attention. "Is that one of…?"

Bauer nodded. He instantly went down on one knee and bowed his head. The action caused the others to do the same.

"Holy space balls," Harper swore under her breath in awe. She was slower to kneel. "What is she doing here? I didn't think they were allowed to leave the compound."

Bauer didn't appear to have an answer.

"Should we…?" Lucien asked.

The crew remained standing. Rick was too mesmerized to move.

The young woman stopped in her progression toward them. She leaned to study the face of one of the agents. A violent shiver racked her body before she pulled away. Leaning to one of the other kneeling men, she ordered, "Shoot him."

The spirit's voice was not as soft as one would expect from an airy being.

The agent took out his blaster and fired without hesitation. The crew jolted at the sound of the weapon's discharge. The condemned agent fell without having put up a fight. No one went to aid him.

"Never mind," Viktor whispered. "Rick, don't you dare piss her off."

Rick saw Viktor pulling his brother as they both kneeled on the ground.

The woman refocused her attention and moved toward them.

"Rick? Do you know this woman?" Dev asked. "She seems to recognize you."

Rick shook his head in denial. The loading dock was quiet. None of the soldiers moved to stand. They kept their eyes down as if afraid to look at the creature.

"Rick, you should kneel. She's one of the eight crystals," Harper said in a reverent tone. He had no idea what that meant.

Rick started to kneel like Harper suggested, but the creature locked eyes with him and lifted her hand. He leaned away when she made a move to touch him. There was something familiar about her features, especially her eyes.

"You have done it," the spirit said, smiling.

Rick glanced to where the dead man lay, unsure if that was a good thing.

"Don't worry about that." She touched his cheek and waited until his eyes met hers. Energy hummed from her fingers. "His darkness needed to be stopped before it ate its way out. Fifty-seven people were saved."

Rick again glanced at the dead man, and the crystal moved to block his view.

"You have done almost all I have asked of you," the woman continued.

"I'm sorry. I think you have the wrong man," Rick said. "I don't know you."

The spirit chuckled as if he was telling a joke.

"I am three," she said. Her skin began to solidify as if finding form. The pink glow about her swirled and lost intensity. It collected into the body of a young girl. She cupped her hand to her mouth and leaned up to whisper, "But you call me Sprout."

Rick fell back into the ship's exterior. His hands shook, and he was sure he might be dreaming. Before him stood the childhood friend he'd held in his arms as she'd bled out. He sank to his knees in disbelief so that his face was level with hers.

All the emotions he felt that day in the forest as a young boy surged within him. He remembered her face, her laugh, her smile, and the way it all faded as blood spurted out of her neck. This was not possible.

"Sprout?" He shook his head in denial. "How? I saw… Are you… a ghost?"

The child's hands cupped his cheeks. The energy in her fingertips had lessened from when she was in spirit form. "You've become even more beautiful than I hoped, my creation."

"What the hell is going on?" Jackson whispered. "Is that Rick's mother?"

"Shh," Raisa shushed him.

Sprout didn't take her eyes off Rick, as if memorizing his face.

"I saw you die," Rick stated.

"I didn't want to do that to you but you saw what you needed to see. You would have looked for me because you are a loyal friend, and I needed you to look for those adventures I planted inside your head. I needed you to use the knowledge I uploaded into your brain to do what must be done. All of that led to this. So many lives disrupted here. Six thousand, two hundred and ninety-eight lives were saved by the actions of you and your crew today—the ones here now, the ones that would have come later, and not counting the babies that would not have been born. I saw this when I met you in the forest." She continued to stroke his cheeks.

Rick could not look away. She mesmerized him, not just with her touch, but with the memories she drew from the depths of his mind. It only raised more questions.

Sprout nodded as if hearing what was swirling in his thoughts. "You were always full of questions. I appeared to your father as the ghost of your mother. I told him to lead you away from my dead body. I told him to make sure you told no one of what you saw, or that you would both die a terrible fate."

His father had done just that. He could almost hear the sound of his father's voice repeating, *"Push it far from your mind, never mention her, never think about her, never go looking."*

"Your father's fate was already written. I knew he would not survive the death of your mother. He did not have inside of him what you have inside of you." Sprout's voice sounded so young and innocent.

No one dared to interrupt Sprout as she spoke. When Rick glanced around, only his crew seemed bold enough to look directly at the girl. Harper snuck a quick peek before averting her gaze.

"I found the stone prisoners you used to talk about," Rick said. "They were on Florencia's Fifth Moon. We freed one, the only one we could save."

Sprout nodded and glanced at Violette. "I know. You brought two sisters together across an impossible lifetime." Sprout's attention did not stay off Rick for very long. "You saved the prince from his own loneliness. Captain Samantha and Prince Falke's children will do great things. You helped Princess Mei's family discover the drug production in the mines. Your actions spread over the universes and stopped a planet from exploding, and you didn't even know it was in danger."

"I did all that?" He slowly lifted his hand to touch Sprout, as she did him. Her face was soft, just like a child's, but this was no young girl. The kind of wisdom that only came with age filled her eyes.

"You all did. Together. In your adventures, you collected the people you needed to assemble along the way. First, by finding a crew, and then by believing in a curse." Sprout looked at Harper. "And you sought adventure and pleasure where you could. I am glad you are finally able to remember her. It was too early before. Don't worry, most of the memories will come back to you in time now that you know they are missing."

"You know about the curse?" Rick asked.

"I whispered it to Zhang An. How else would you have found your true family?" She giggled, a girlish sound. "Besides, what better reward for all you have done, and will do, than to find love?"

Rick glanced at Harper.

"Um, excuse me, crystal, lady, um, Lady Crystal Sprout?" Lucien lifted his hand. "Not everyone on the crew was cursed."

Sprout glanced at him. "Didn't you find the sisters?"

Viktor and Lucien shook their heads in denial.

"They're around here somewhere," Sprout dismissed, again turning to Rick. She stared at him, smiling, not saying a word, as if time had no meaning.

"So, what now?" Rick asked, unsure how to take the news that everything in his life was tied to his childhood friend. There were threads spreading out over time and space, connecting him to this moment. He'd always felt that some greater power didn't want him dead. Was Samantha's saving him, the pirate life, the curse, finding Harper, all to serve this moment? To be in this place at this time to free these people? If this was his life's purpose, what next? Did the fates have no more use for him?

"So many questions swirling," Sprout whispered. "My tasks for you are done. I can ask no more. I release you."

Now that he knew the truth, Rick wasn't sure he wanted to be released from his life having a purpose.

"Don't look so worried. Find your own adventures. There are plenty of people out there who need help." She glanced at Harper. "Take her with you. I'm sure she'll have some ideas."

Rick looked at Harper. Her head had lifted, and she stared at him. Like every other time he was near her, his heart beat a little faster. "Only if she wants to stay with me."

Sprout furrowed her brow and went to where Harper kneeled. "You should tell him."

Harper glanced at Rick before turning to Bauer.

Sprout grabbed Harper's jaw, her little fingers gripping tight. Her body began to glow brighter, and tiny lights danced over her. "Tell him. Don't worry about Agent Bauer or the agency. Make up your own mind."

Harper took a deep breath and gazed at Rick. "I love you. I want to be with you. But——"

"Agent Bauer," Sprout cut her off. Her body grew and she retook her ghostly form before gliding to the man. "Harper has to stay with Rick now."

Rick pulled Harper to stand next to him. He wrapped his arms around her and held her close.

"Those aren't the orders I've received," Bauer said. "I'm——"

"The fate of three, no, tell them seven planets are in the balance. Good planets, too, not those industrial smog smelly planets like Rayvik." Sprout ordered. "You're to fix their ship and let these people be on their way."

Bauer nodded. "I'll see to it."

"We need to relocate all of these people, and you need to report to Zoxin to deal with the Red Guard," Sprout ordered. "Bring extra boots with you."

"Will they really just let us leave?" Violette asked.

"Sounds like it," Jackson answered.

"I'm going to find Alexis." Lochlann boarded the ship. No one stopped him.

"I didn't think we were going to make it out of this one," Rick said.

"I didn't either." Harper didn't take her eyes from him. "I can't believe your childhood friend is one of the crystals."

"I still don't know what that means." Rick couldn't help himself. He held her tighter.

"Now, please, Agent Bauer," Sprout said.

Bauer stood and began shouting orders to bring down transport ships to load the workers and to have engineers and mechanics board the *Bound Virgin*. The once silent room suddenly filled with movement.

"He's one of the good ones," Sprout said of the agent as he did as she'd commanded. "He's facing a scorching path, but he's Killian so it's fine." She leaned forward and whispered. "Don't be jealous, Rick, but if he succeeds, he'll save five more lives than you so far. Unless you choose to continue your work."

"Hold on," Lucien called as he moved to go after Bauer. "Not the sisters. Don't load the sisters. You heard the lady. We need to take them with us."

Viktor hesitated, glancing at Sprout before following his brother.

Sprout watched them leave before saying, "I might have forgotten to tell them the sisters have already stowed away on your ship." She waved a hand in dismissal. "They'll figure it out."

Since he hadn't realized he'd been on some special mission set into motion during childhood, he hardly knew how to continue it unless it was to keep being himself. That would be easy enough.

Sprout smiled at him, not seeming to notice the fact he embraced Harper. She reached between them and touched his face. Her fingers hummed with ethereal energy.

"You may be my most favorite thing." Sprout tapped his nose. "You still have it in there."

"What?" Harper asked.

"You feel it," Sprout dismissed Harper's question.

"Yeah, what?" Rick wondered if there was another surprise lurking in his mind. Between his childhood friend and the woman he loved, his brain had been messed with more than he cared to think about.

"Life." Sprout pressed closer, her glowing eyes focusing in on his. "Purity."

At the word *purity*, Jackson and Dev both snorted back laughter.

"Yeah, Rick's as pure as new Sintaz snow," Jackson muttered.

"Shut your holes," Violette whispered. "Don't make her mad."

"I think she's pretty," Raisa answered.

Sprout pulled back, glancing at Raisa and Violette before shaking her head like an exasperated mother dealing with children. As if coming out of her daze, she frowned at Harper. "What is that nagging question rattling around inside you?"

"No question. I love him. I'm sure of it. No question. I want to be with Rick. Forever." Harper's arms pulled tighter as if afraid Sprout would take him from her.

When Rick looked at the crystal, he felt calm, connected. Witnessing the faces of the others, he saw they were more apprehensive of the powerful being. Even the agents were moving quickly past them, not making eye contact. Two men hauled the dead agent into a transport coffin, while a third cleaned the mess.

"No, of course you're in love with him. That was true from the first moment." Sprout looked pointedly at Rick. "You don't remember, but you felt it too." She then turned back to Harper. "Defect. Defect." She waved her hands beside her head. "Ask already."

"When we landed the intake guard said I was defective and wouldn't take me as a worker." Harper faced the crystal while keeping an arm wrapped around Rick to keep him close.

"That?" Sprout arched a brow. She glanced over Harper. "Oh."

At the flat intonation, Harper stiffened.

"Oh!" Sprout's tone changed to one of surprise. "A little Rick." She pressed her hand against Harper's belly. Harper stiffened, her eyes widening.

Rick stared at Harper's stomach. A baby? His baby? There were many adventures he'd dreamed up in his mind, but fatherhood was never one of them. What did he know about children besides the fact he'd been one? Though, he also never thought he'd find a love like Harper, either.

"But I have… shots," Harper mumbled, in just as much shock as he was over the news.

"Hello, little star," Sprout said to the stomach.

Harper's widened eyes met his and it looked like Sprout was petting his son.

"Holy… did she say Rick…?" Jackson asked.

"A baby!" Raisa squealed and clapped her hands.

Sprout withdrew her hand. She grinned at Rick. "He'll be a handful but raise him right, and he'll have it inside of him just like you do."

"I can't believe——" Dev began.

"No!" Sprout shouted, lifting her finger to the side.

Dev stopped talking in surprise.

An agent carrying a box of engine parts paused on his way up the loading plank and held very still.

"There will be no trackers built into the ship. Get it out of here," Sprout ordered. The agent nodded. She gave one last look at Rick, "Until the future, old friend."

Her body dissipated as she whisked away, and they heard one last shout, "Agent Bauer, a word!"

"I can't believe it," Dev repeated.

"That I'm a hero?" Rick asked with a cocky grin.

"No," Dev denied. "I don't think anyone used the word hero."

"You heard her. I saved like ten thousand people today," Rick answered. "That makes me a hero."

"You're still a space cadet," Jackson quipped.

"Six thousand, two hundred and ninety-eight lives," Raisa corrected the total.

"Is it that you can't believe that I'm pregnant?"

Harper hesitated before looking up at Rick. "I can't believe it either."

"No. I can believe that. I know how babies are made," Dev said.

"He sure does." Lucien appeared next to Dev. "Just ask the Murkernals."

Dev scowled at him.

Lucien reached up to slap Dev's back, completely unconcerned by the look. "Has anyone seen two sexy sisters walking around?"

Dev pointed across the loading docks toward a door.

"Thanks, big guy." Lucien ran in the direction he indicated.

"Sprout said they're on the ship." Raisa pointed a thumb over her shoulders.

"I know," Dev answered, smiling.

"A baby was bound to happen to one of us sooner rather than later," Violette said. "Congratulations, both of you."

"Little Star Rick Hayes," Rick grinned. He slipped his hand onto Harper's belly. "I could get used to that."

"Oh, no," Harper shook her head. "We are not naming this baby Star."

"But you heard what the crystal said," Rick protested.

"Yeah, what's with the eight crystals thing?" Jackson asked.

Harper looked in the direction Sprout had disappeared to. "They're a group of eight humanoid psychics who provide vital intelligence to the HIA. I've known about them, but this is the first time I've seen one. When they are certain about something, they're never wrong, and when they give orders, we're told to listen. Apparently, there was a planetary-ending event they tried to stop, but politics got in the way. Many Jagranst lives were lost. The way I've heard it, the crystals went into a compound and held themselves hostage until they had supreme authority to act on their predictions. They still live in the compound, away from humans, taking in the information we gather and analyzing it. I've never heard of one leaving. We're not supposed to talk about them outside of briefings."

"Told you I was awesome," Rick said. "You're lucky to be friends with someone as connected as me."

"What was it you couldn't believe?" Violette asked her husband.

"That Rick behaved himself, was respectful, and didn't have one smartass thing to say to the ghost lady," Dev answered.

"Hey, guys, you might want to get on here and supervise these repairs. The HIA is trying to access our systems." Lochlann rushed down the loading plank to say between clenched teeth, "*All* our systems."

"I've got the VR programs," Dev said to Jackson.

"I'll take care of the secret lab," Violette added.

Dev and Violette both ran onto the ship.

"My molecular gastro-spectrometer." Raisa grabbed Jackson's hand and pulled him behind her as she hurried to go on board. "You can repair it, but no one better touch the settings!"

When they were left relatively alone with only a few dozen passing agents, Rick cupped Harper's face. He leaned to kiss her, pausing just long enough to say, "Rocket Rick Hayes?"

Harper laughed into his kiss, her lips lingering on his. When she pulled back, she said, "Not my son."

"Comet Rick Hayes?"

"No." She tugged at his hand. "Don't we have some ship files to protect?"

"Yeah, but..." Rick grinned as she drew him behind her. "Okay, how about Blaster? Oh, or, Firefight? Player Rick Hayes?"

"You're officially banned from naming our child," Harper stated.

He stopped walking as they entered the ship corridor and pulled her into his arms. "I love you,

Harper. I promise I'll do whatever I have to keep you and our child safe."

"I love you, too, Rick. And we're going to raise our son right, like Sprout said," Harper stated, "and that means doing what we do best—adventures and saving people."

"You are the perfect woman." Rick grinned as he lifted her off the ground and spun in a small circle.

She laughed as he lowered her against his body, letting her feel the unmistakable press of his arousal.

"Think they'll be doing repairs in the supply closet?" she asked before furrowing her brow. "Unless we can't get open the door without electricity?"

"I'll pry it open." He grabbed her hand and began jogging down the corridor, looking for any place they could slip into for privacy.

EPILOGUE

Bound Virgin, Larceny Casino Docking Line

"How much longer?" Harper rubbed her hand over the small bump of her pregnancy.

Rick had the viewing screen pulled up to show a long line of ships waiting to enter the casino docks. The HIA had done a great job repairing the vessel. It still looked like a cobbled together piece of junk, but it ran beautifully. Though, they had undone all his customized rewiring, so he was still trying to change it back to the way he liked it.

He leaned over from his pilot's seat and placed his hand over his son. "Hello, little Player."

"Still, no," Harper stated, brushing his hand away.

"Don't worry, son, I'll make sure you have an amazing name."

She pointed at the screen. "How long?"

"Hour. I hacked their frequency and they're having an issue with a Dokka freighter." Rick glanced to the line of ships on the viewing screen before turning his attention back to Harper's stomach. "And how is my beautiful wife today?"

"Better, now that I gave the baby what he wanted," she said.

"Which was?" Rick arched a brow.

"Bacon. He freaking loves bacon." She moved to sit on his lap. "I can't stop craving it, and I know I don't like it but then I taste it and it's all I want to eat."

Rick adjusted himself beneath her and wrapped his arms lightly around her waist. "One of the transmissions we're monitoring had news about your old friend, Bucky, this morning. He's apparently been found alive on some fueling port. They're bringing him to stand trial for the bionic factory crimes with his parents. That footage Bauer leaked—"

"Alexis said the card game starts in six hours," Ruva interrupted as she appeared in the doorway. "She has a ticket for Jackson to play. If he loses the secondary plan will be for Lochlann and Dev to free the woman from stasis. They could be coming in hot."

Ruva and her sister Alke were in the process of a long courtship with Lucien and Viktor. They looked identical, and the crew could only tell them apart by the way Ruva wore her hair, wound around the crown of her head. Though, if the sisters were ever to change things up, they'd be in trouble.

"I'm supposed to ask how long until we dock," she said.

"Hour," Harper and Rick answered in unison.

"Thanks. I'll let everyone know." She started to leave, only to come back. "Do either of you know how to repair the VR program with all the women? They're naked and missing heads. I thought it would be nice to fix it, generate clothes for them, and see what this mansion game is all about. Could be a fun distraction."

Rick bit back a laugh. "Sorry, I don't know. You should ask Viktor."

"Oh, okay." Ruva smiled as she left.

"What was that about?" Harper leaned her head on his shoulder as she nestled into his embrace.

"Viktor tried to scan a copy of the Galaxy Play-mates VR program back on Nozando. With the electrical issues we were having after that trip, I don't think it loaded completely." Rick laughed harder. "I didn't want to be the one to tell her that the ladies probably did not come with clothes. And the mansion is not the kind of game she thinks it is."

Harper's laugh joined his. "You're telling me we have a VR with headless strippers?"

"Hey, it's not mine. I didn't do it. I have all the woman I need right here." Rick stroked his wife's hair. "And I think they prefer to be called dancers."

"But you can access it, right? The program?" Harper asked.

"Sure, I guess I could." Rick leaned back to study her face. "Do you want me to?"

"Mansion full of games? Tell me that doesn't sound fun." She pressed her lips to his in a deep and telling kiss. His body instantly responded. "We'll give those headless dancers a show they'll never forget."

Rick stood, easing her gently to the ground. He pushed the ship's comm and said, "Sorry folks, looks like another delay. Going to be closer to two—"

"Three," Harper inserted.

"—*three* hours before it's our turn to dock. Darn those Dokka freighters. Don't worry, we'll make the card game on time." He turned off the comm and hit the autopilot before pulling her against him to kiss her deeply. "I love you. You are my everything."

"Prove it, my love. Show me." She gave him a

playfully naughty look and crooked her finger for him to follow.

"Gladly." Rick swept her into his arms as he strode toward the VR to satisfy his wife.

The End

Space Lords Series
His Frost Maiden
His Fire Maiden
His Metal Maiden
His Earth Maiden
His Woodland Maiden

Qurilixen Lords

Dragon Prince

Grier's fiery passion for Salena might be everything his dragon ever wanted but loving her might just lead to the destruction of everything he's trying to save.

With all that is happening in his land, the upcoming shifter mating ceremony is the least of Grier's concerns. Even though he is heir prince of the dragon-shifters, he doesn't have the authority needed to help the humans stranded in dragon territory, nor can he banish those who ruthlessly control them. Yet honor demands he finds an opportunity to intervene, and he hopes that doing so won't start a war the shifters can't win. Discovering his destined mate couldn't have come at a worse time.

Salena knows what it is like to be a pawn of the Federation. They might have kidnapped her and brought her to this strange territory, but she will never do what they want of her... what everyone wants of her. The last thing the fugitive needs is the very public attention of a fierce dragon prince claiming they're fated by the gods—even if the sexy man makes her burn in more ways than one.

Chapter One Excerpt

He was not the king, not yet.

He could not help the people before him.

He could not banish those who needed to be ejected off his world.

Grier didn't know how to explain to his royal parents and the Draig elders that this wasn't the same world anymore. They clung to the past with an almost delusional need, as if, by willing it hard enough, everything would return to the ways of their youth. Hope and determination did not change reality. Qurilixen was no longer the primitive oasis of farmers and ceffyl herders whose biggest worry was protecting the ore mines from alien attacks or guarding the borderlands against their feral Var neighbors.

If only that were still the reality, when dragon-shifters and cat-shifters were the only kinds on this planet. Such times seemed easy compared to now.

Grier was probably oversimplifying matters. His father had warned him more than once to be careful about minimizing the past. The old days had not been as easy as Grier was wont to believe, and there were many things he did not know. That may be true, but he knew the problems of here and now.

Grier gazed down from the cliffside watchtower at the alien city sprawled over the valley below. There was something calming about sitting on the circular roof, at a height so great that none of the new residents of the planet could reach it. Locals had nicknamed the settlement below Shelter City because they meant it to be a temporary shelter for their visitors. That was over thirty years ago.

The top of the tower that surrounded a spire was flat, wide enough for him to sit, but the roof slats at his feet angled downward. He felt the wind, smelled the fresh air, heard only the barest hint of shouts from below.

The city was not supposed to have lasted as long as it had. Qurilixen was to be a short resting place where the people regained their strength after the destruction of their world and recovered from a virus that killed almost their entire population. His father, King Ualan, and the Var cat-shifting King

Kirill, could no longer turn away hundreds of people in need, any more than they could have killed the aliens themselves. When they had agreed to partner with the Federation to save the Cysgodians, there had been invisible strings attached to the deal that had only revealed themselves over time.

Grier gazed over one such string. Until that moment, the shifters had kept their planet from any dealings with the Federation and free of its rules. They did not want to be part of the Federation Alliance. Now they were in a questionable gray area. The Federation claimed squatters' rights because they had dominion over the makeshift city, and the shifters refused to agree that city was anything more than a temporary settlement—to do so would be to accept the alliance.

They were at a standstill. The real victims of this political battle were the people caught in the middle. If the dragon prince could have his way, he'd funnel the people out of the city and allow them to choose their path—whether it was to stay on the planet or leave for space. No one's destiny should be decided by a dictatorship.

The cluster of metal and stone buildings, built in a hurry and falling over time, created the portion of the city that filled the valley. Canvas flapped in the wind, giving shade from the constant daylight of the planet. This is where the Federation kept their poor, which was almost every citizen of the city. Shifters had no say in the alien hierarchy.

Grier wanted to change that. Politics would not let him. He hated these politics.

The shifters did not have poor, or at least they hadn't before the Cysgodians came. Dragon-shifters took care of their own. If a child was orphaned, there was always a family willing to give them a new home. His cousin, Mirek, had not been blessed with children but had more sons than the rest of them combined from taking in those in need of a family. If someone needed food, someone fed them. Everyone worked, and everyone thrived. They considered it a matter of honor.

It was this sentiment that had caused his parents to take in so many off-worlders when they'd known it would strain their resources. Scientists had been convinced the blue radiation from one of Qurilixen's three suns had the healing properties the Cysgodians needed to recover. Besides, at the time, there was nowhere else for the residents to go.

But then, the city grew, too fast to be natural. They discovered others were being brought to the sanctuary—first three more; then twelve; then a shipful dropped off during the one night a year when darkness covered the planet, and the dragons had been occupied with their sacred mating cere-monies. That is how Shelter City now held more than the original Cysgodians, though they still used the term to describe the people there. *Cysgod* meant shelter in the Draig language, so it made sense.

By the time they made the discovery, it was too late. The people had dispersed into Shelter City and to round them up would have meant full-on attacks. None of the shifters wanted a war. What they wanted was the Federation gone as it was their fault this was happening. They had taken advantage of the elders' good-hearted natures and the Cysgodians' desperation.

Grier was not as soft-hearted as the elders. He couldn't be. He knew in order for his people to survive, he would have to make hard choices, ones he did not want to make.

Looking at his hands, he traced an old scar he'd received in battle training as a youth.

"Battles are not meant to be easy. They are meant to be won," had been the lesson his uncle Zoran, commander of the Draig army, wanted them to learn. Zoran was still a hard taskmaster to this day. Grier had received the scar from Zoran's daughter, Grace.

Fights did not scare him. Losing his people did. For better or worse, the Cysgodians were now his people, and they needed freed from the Federation's rule. Only then could the shifters start truly absorbing them into Qurilixen society if that is what the aliens wanted. As it was, crime and discontentment were escalating.

Above the city of metal and stone were structures of a different nature. They were evenly spaced buildings along the ridge of a mountain, identical and just as they had been since the Federation put them up thirty years earlier.

A large stone building towered over it all, across the valley from his watchtower perch but low enough that he could see the roof. The rectangular structure stretched along the length of the city. Metal arches slashed over the top. That is where the city officials stayed. It was where his parents and ambassador cousin were now, discussing the many issues that arose from this ever-growing nest of malcontents.

Suddenly, a wave of heat hit his back, propelling his body down the side of the roof. A roar of flames filled the sky over his head. He dug his heels against the surface even as his hands flailed to grab something solid. The slats of the roof clattered under his boots as he tried to stop his fall. It didn't work. As he flew over the side of the tower, he managed to grab hold of the edge with one hand. He swung violently so that his back struck the stone side. Another roar of fire filled the air.

He took a deep breath, ignoring the pounding of his heart as he gained control of his body.

Kicking the side of the building, he propelled himself around, gripping the roof's edge even as he released his anchored hand long enough to change his hold so that his wrist wouldn't break.

Grier did not hang long. He used his toe to launch from the side and his arm strength to lift his head over the edge of the rooftop to look at his attacker.

Grace peeked at him from the other side of his resting spot, hiding her naked body. Her light brown eyes shone with mischief. His cousin was pretty and would have appeared as regal as any queen if not for the fact she'd just tried to firebomb him off the side of the tower. Her brown hair flew around her head. She grinned down at him. "Let me borrow your shirt."

Grier dropped his weight, kicked off the side of the building a second time and flung his body upward. With much effort, he climbed onto the roof and made his way toward the top. Sitting with his back to his cousin, he took off his shirt and held it behind him. The cooler air hit his naked chest, and he breathed deeply. "Do I even want to ask where you left your clothes?"

He felt Grace take the shirt. Seconds later she was sitting next to him, wearing it. Her bare feet tapped on the roof slats as she propped her arms on her knees. Grier was glad she was his cousin. In any form, she was dangerous. As a fighter, she was fierce. As a dragon, she was terrifying. As a woman, she was stunningly beautiful. As a cousin, she liked to fly up behind him and fireball him off the side of a tower for fun.

"Anything interesting happening in the village of discontent?" she asked, sounding restless.

He ignored her question and instead asked one of his own. "Does Uncle Zoran know you are flying around the forbidden valley?"

Grier already knew the answer.

"My father still thinks of me as I was at twenty years old and wants me to sit where he can see me at all times. He doesn't like me to come here. He thinks it isn't safe." Grace adjusted her position a little. "I don't know what he thinks will happen."

Grier had only known two female dragons in his life—his grandmother and Grace. And his grandmother had died years ago.

Anyone who didn't know the warrior prince would have seen Zoran's treatment of his daughter as contradictory. Perhaps it was because dragons rarely had female children. On the one hand, Grace was a dragon who should be trained for battle like a dragon. And yet, she was also female and dragon males tended to treat females like they were delicate and to be protected—which was funny on many levels. Since Zoran's mother, their grandmother, had also been a rare female dragon he should have known better. And, Zoran's wife, Princess Pia was one tough human.

"Cysgodians could shoot you from the sky. The Federation could capture you and smuggle you off the planet in the dead of night to do experiments on you," Grier listed, mostly to be annoying. "Var marsh farmer could try to mate you and set you up as queen of the stills. The Var prince—"

"Stop agreeing with my father." Grace's eyes flashed gold with warning.

Rare dragon birth, a dragon grandmother, a mother who could kickass with the best of them, four younger brothers, countless male cousins, and a commander father? Yeah, it stood to reason Grace would be a little wild.

"He loves you," Grier said. "His actions all come down to that."

Perhaps Zoran's reactions were something Grier would only understand when he too was a father. And, perhaps still, maybe his uncle's protectiveness had something to do with how his daughter was always rebelling.

"He also doesn't like it when we call Shelter City the forbidden valley." Grace gave a small laugh, clearly wanting to change the subject. "Though, he wouldn't want me saying the village of discontent either."

Grier patted her shoulder. "So, you rebel and fly up here where he can't reach you? Careful, or he'll have you chained to the ground again."

Grace smiled, not worried. She'd been escaping her father's numerous guards since they were children. "He left my idiot brothers to keep me company. Slipping away from the palace was not difficult."

Grier laughed as he realized what was going on. "The Var princes are coming by the palace today, aren't they?"

"I don't want to talk about it," Grace grumbled.

Grier arched a brow and teased, "I would think you'd be excited to spend time with your future—"

"I *will* throw you off this tower," she warned. "Prince Korbin is not my future anything."

"Careful, little one, that is war talk." Grier wasn't concerned. Grace had been privately ranting about her betrothal to the future cat-shifting king since she could talk. Though, she said nothing publicly. Pia had wanted nothing to do with that part of the shifter peace treaty, and he once overheard his aunt telling Grace that time would dissolve that nonsense. It had not.

"Careful, *bloated* one," she mocked his nickname for her, "or I'll tell Queen Rigan next time I see her that you're planning on hiding from the mating festival again this year. You know the people would feel better if the future king settled and began the next generation. Such security in the future would go a long way toward keeping the peace our parents fought so hard to secure. There are factions on both sides keen on restarting the old wars to decide once and for all who is the superior shifter race—cats or dragons."

Grier took a deep breath. She was not wrong. Add to that the political unrest surrounding the intruders below, and it wouldn't take much to incite some battle over this or that.

"I don't know why you resist," Grace teased. "You would have such cute little dragon babies."

Grier picked at the crystal sewn into the thick leather bracelet on his arm. When he met his mate, the stone was supposed to glow and let him know that fate had arrived. It kept the guesswork out of marrying, and for that he was grateful. Who had time to test out relationships? Frankly, the alien method of dating multiple people sounded tiring.

"I am not like my parents," Grier said when she continued to look at him expectantly. "I do not wish to marry. It is too much of a distraction, and I need my mind focused elsewhere."

It wasn't the complete truth. He didn't go to the mating ceremonies because he didn't want the gods to bless him yet. Of course, he wanted to marry. Who didn't want to find the other half of their soul?

But if a battle were to come, in any of its many threatening forms, a wife would be a weakness he couldn't afford. There were stories of how some of his aunts had been kidnapped by the previous Var king to be used as leverage, but that was decades ago.

"On that we can agree," Grace said. She did not wear her crystal. They never spoke of it, but he assumed it was because her fate had been sealed since she was born, and to know anything else would have been too much for her heart to bear. "We are definitely not our parents."

"Besides, if anything happens to me, I have plenty of cousins who can take the throne." He nudged her arm.

"Don't trust your brothers to do the job?"

Grier laughed. "Do you want Creed ruling this planet?"

"Fair point," Grace said of Grier's youngest brother. "Though Altair might—"

"Order all dragons from the sky to live like the old ways?" he inserted.

"Right, never mind." Grace held up her hands. "It's settled. You have to marry and have many children."

"Or you could take the job. What do you say? Queen Grace and King Korbin could unite the shifter people once and for all. You have Grandmother Mede's fierce dragon heart. You will be the first to rule both dragons and cat-shifters."

"Not on your life." She closed her eyes and lifted her face toward the two yellow suns. The blue sun wasn't high in the sky at the moment. She gave a wistful sigh. "Do you remember our parents' faces when they realized all their dragon babies could fly and spout flames? I think our grandmother was the only excited one."

Before their generation, only the rare female dragons flew and breathed flames, and only under extreme duress.

"That's because Queen Mede was the only dragon who had ever flown or breathed fire in Qurilixen's history before we came along." Grier smiled as he remembered their shared past. It had been what felt like a hundred years ago, but the memory was a fond one. "Rune panicked and became stuck in that tree, and you tried to help him but ended up setting the tree on fire, which lit up the barracks and took out the palace guards' housing. Half of them bunked in the palace dining hall and the other half slept on the practice field."

Grace laughed. "Then they caught us trying to set dried solarflowers on fire."

"You and Kane were trying to set fire to them," he corrected. "The rest of us were wrongfully blamed."

"Don't complain. Grandfather pretended to punish us, but really let us camp out in the royal offices all night as he told us scary stories about the portal travels our ancestors took to leave the evil persecutors." Grace closed her eyes and smiled. "He stole those biscuit things from our grandmother, and a tray of chocolate. We ate so much we had upset stomachs for two days."

"Great-grandmother's sugar biscuit recipe that she brought with her from the Florencian moons. I haven't had those for years." The wind whipped through Grier's hair, tousling it around his head.

"I miss them," Grace admitted. King Llyr and Queen Mede were not only missed by their grand-children, but by their people. "No matter what happened, they always defended us. Grandmother was the only one who could understand what is inside me."

Silence came over them, and he followed her gaze upward to the sky. The wide open space called to something deep inside him. It stirred his blood with excitement and tempted him with the freedom it offered.

"Do you remember when Jaxx convinced us we could fly into space if we went high enough?" he asked.

Grace again laughed. "We thought we were so tough. Maxen passed out and free fell to the ground.

It was a miracle Lantos caught him. Then Aunt Nadja grounded us all to the castle while she tried to figure out how our shifting abilities had mutated so differently from our parents'. I think they wanted to temper them back to keep us safe."

"You can't hold back evolution," Grier said. "We are what nature and the blue sun intended us to be."

"What do you think the radiation will do to their genetics?" Grace nodded down to the city.

The blue sun gave the shifters strength and a long life; it also had made the odds of having a female baby extremely rare. It had taken generations before the dragon gene had mutated into what they were now.

"What do you think their grandchildren will become?" she continued to muse.

"Space explorers?" Grier hoped. "Then they could fly off this planet for good and finally be free of the Federation Military."

"Perhaps." Grace laughed. Then, gesturing toward the rectangular buildings, she said, "What do you think they do all day in there? I want to freeze time and walk around those buildings to see all their horrible secrets."

"Nothing useful." Unable to stop himself, he grinned at her and again patted her shoulder. "Kind of like you."

He slid his hand from her shoulder down to the small of her back and launched her from the tower with one push. She screamed in surprise, flailing her arms as her body sailed over the edge of the roof before dropping. The sound of her voice became smaller as she fell down the side of the cliff.

Grier settled into his original spot, overlooking the city. It was almost a shame to lose the shirt. He liked the fit of that one.

A whoosh of air sounded from below and then another, the rhythm steadily growing louder before his cousin's dragon form appeared. She was a slender creature in shifted form, smaller than her male counterparts, but what she lacked in brute strength she made up for in gracefulness. Her wings flapped slowly, holding her body suspended in air.

Grace roared fire into the sky in a show of mock anger before turning her mouth toward him. He braced himself for the flames, ready to shift if he had to protect his fragile human skin. She inhaled a deep breath, but instead of flames, a playful ring of smoke came from her mouth to drift around him. Part of the circle broke apart as it hit the tower.

She propelled herself backward, circling in the air before diving away from him. He could tell by the way she flew that she had only come here to waste the hours until the Var princes returned home. The royal family couldn't expect her to entertain if she was nowhere to be found.

Shouts sounded from below. Grier narrowed his gaze to focus his vision as his eyes shifted to make out the details. A mob of people flowed through the central street of the city, clashing with a second mob. The people converged like two swollen streams, spilling over into the side streets.

He sighed heavily. The fighting was not unusual.

Grier resisted the urge to swoop down and drag them apart with his talons. Instead, he went to the side of the roof, grabbed a knob that had been placed at the edge, and then dropped over the side. He swung around into an opening at the top of the tower and landed on the stone floor. There, he pulled off his boots and pants. Once naked, he went to the window and dove from the tower. His body fell for a few seconds before he let the shift have him. The transformation was painful, but it was an old pain that he had long ago learned to disregard.

Grier's bones cracked as his body extended, and his skin hardened with protective brown armor. Wings ripped out of his back, lifting him before he hit the ground. The transformation finished as he was suspended in the air. A long tail grew from the bottom of his spine only to have a spade sharpen the end. Deadly talons replaced his nails. His beard disappeared, and his jaw popped, making room for sharp teeth.

The wind caressed the full length of his form. For a moment, the feeling of freedom rushed through him, the animal instinct desperate to take over his reason. The beast was as much a part of him as the man. He pushed the feeling down, concentrating on what needed to be done.

Grier dove toward the fight in the street, roaring before sending a burst of flames into the sky. He was careful not to hit any of the structures, but it was enough to get the people's attention. He swooped over the epicenter of the hostility. Screams pierced the air as people ran away from him to take cover.

Grier roared once in warning before lifting himself higher and flying away. Then, because the freedom of flight felt so damned good, he circled the entire city a few times before heading back to the tower. He wanted to keep soaring but forced himself to land on the roof.

His body contracted as he shifted halfway back to his human form to stand as a dragon-man. It was in this half shift that he looked like his father's dragon. The tail disappeared as did the talons on his feet. The talons on his fingers shortened, still sharp and deadly but more like fingernails. In this form, the dragon impulses were easier to control. He used his dragon vision to look down at the valley below.

The fighting had dispersed, and the streets cleared of both mobs. The fray was over.

The thick armor of Grier's skin protected his naked body as he slid down the side of the roof. He again grabbed the knob and swung down into the tower window. His clothes were piled on the floor. Now safely inside, the armored flesh softened into human skin, and he again stood as a man.

The tight pants felt a little constrictive after a shift. His sensitive skin tingled. Grier leaned against the partition wall as he tugged on his boots before rounding the corner to the other side. The wall acted like a windshield for the landing room.

Stacks of plain linen shirts and pants had little by way of style but were cheap to make. They served as replacement clothes for the flyers, and he took a shirt from the top of the pile. Their full dragon bodies expanded beyond the confines of clothing. It was a little hard to fit a giant pair of wings into a tunic shirt, and they'd kept ending up naked in inopportune situations.

His aunt Olena had been the one to suggest the caches around the kingdom. Out of all the elders, she alone never tried to curb their wild ways. It wasn't a secret in their family that she'd been some-what of a space pirate in her youth. She used to hide treasures in the forest for them to hunt down.

Grace had set his thoughts toward the past when

he needed to think about the present. The tension in Shelter City had already spilled over into the rest of the planet. The little skirmish below was bad, but it was hardly the worst. Some of the residents were trying to migrate, especially those who'd been born since their arrival.

The Federation didn't like that. In fact, they had forbidden Cysgodians from leaving the city limits.

The Cysgodians' desire to be part of the Quril-ixian culture wasn't an issue for the shifters. Dragons would always do the honorable thing and these people needed a place to live.

He gripped the shirt in his hands as he took the winding path down the stairs. There was little light to see by, but his shifted eyes didn't need help to navigate the way down. Even though the fight was broken up, he should go to the city and find out what had started it.

A soft glow caught his attention, and he turned around to see who followed him. No one was there. He looked down the steps—again, nothing unusual. It was then he realized what caused the glow.

The crystal on his wrist had begun to pulsate with a soft light.

Grier held very still, unable to believe what was happening. He took another step down, then stopped, unsure what he should do. How could his mating crystal be glowing if he was alone in the tower?

He was alone, wasn't he?

Did he really want to find the answer to that question?

"Show yourself," he ordered.

Silence.

His crystal was only meant to glow if he was close to his mate. It was the belief of his people. When they were born, their fathers dove to the bottom of Crystal Lake and chose a crystal. That stone stayed with them until they married. No one was one hundred percent sure how it worked, but they knew that it did. There was no questioning the will of the gods.

"By order of the prince, show yourself," he commanded.

His heartbeat quickened. Had the gods heard him tell his cousin he had no wish to marry? Had they taken offense to his rejection of their gifts and this was their answer to his blasphemy?

Grier ran down the stairs. He couldn't be alone with a glowing crystal. It would mean he was cursed. There was no other explanation.

"Who is there?" Desperation made the dragon's gruff nature enter his voice.

He rushed out the tower, hearing the weight of the wood door slam shut behind him. The rocky landscape was empty as Grier ran around the base of the tower to see if a woman hid from him. His feet slipped as he came close to the edge of the cliff. Pebbles fell down the side, clanking to punctuate how alone he was.

"Please, someone be there," he whispered into the wind. "Where are you? Show yourself."

The glow of his crystal faded. He lifted his arm, pointing the bracelet in every direction to see if the crystal would reactivate. It was over.

In those brief seconds, everything changed.

Grier forgot about the village squabble. How could he think of such things now? He'd received an answer to his offhanded comment to Grace. He would be forever alone.

The gods had cursed him for his arrogance.

To find out more about Michelle's books visit
www.MichellePillow.com

Want to read the connected series?
Check out the first book in the connected series
installments.

Dragon Lords: Barbarian Prince
Lords of the Var®: The Savage King
Space Lords: His Frost Maiden
Captured by a Dragon-Shifter: Determined Prince
Galaxy Alien Mail Order Brides: Spark
Dynasty Lords: Seduction of the Phoenix
Qurilixen Lords: Dragon Prince

PLEASE LEAVE A REVIEW

THANK YOU FOR READING!

Please take a moment to share your thoughts by leaving a review.

Be sure to check out Michelle's other titles at

www.michellepillow.com

9 781625 012371